FIFE COUNCIL LIBRARIES

FB0

D1645730

THE ADVENTURES OF JACK BRENIN

BOOK TWO

Glasruhen Gate

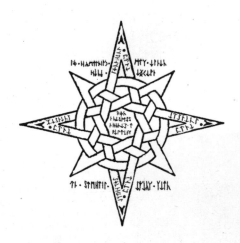

ABOUT THE AUTHOR

Catherine Cooper was a primary school teacher for 29 years before deciding she'd love to write for children. She is the author of four books. Catherine's love of history, myths and legends and the Shropshire countryside around where lives shine through her charming stories. Catherine Cooper's *The Golden Acorn* was the overall winner of the 2010 Brit Writers' Award.

THE ADVENTURES OF JACK BRENIN

BOOK TWO

Glasruhen Gate

CATHERINE COOPER

ILLUSTRATIONS BY
RON COOPER and CATHERINE COOPER

infiniteideas

Copyright text © Catherine Cooper, 2010
Copyright illustrations © Ron Cooper and Catherine Cooper 2010
The right of Catherine Cooper to be identified as the author of this
book has been asserted in accordance with the Copyright,
Designs and Patents Act 1988.

First published in 2010 by Pengridion Books
This edition 2011
Infinite Ideas Limited
36 St Giles
Oxford
OX1 3LD
United Kingdom
www.infideas.com

All rights reserved. Except for the quotation of small passages for the
purposes of criticism or review, no part of this publication may be
reproduced, stored in a retrieval system or transmitted in any form or by
any means, electronic, mechanical, photocopying, recording, scanning or
otherwise, except under the terms of the Copyright, Designs and Patents
Act 1988 or under the terms of a licence issued by the Copyright Licensing
Agency Ltd, 90 Tottenham Court Road, London W1T 4LP, UK, without
the permission in writing of the publisher. Requests to the publisher
should be addressed to the Permissions Department, Infinite Ideas
Limited, 36 St Giles, Oxford, OX1 3LD, UK,
or faxed to +44 (0) 1865 514777.

A CIP catalogue record for this book is available from the British Library

ISBN 978-1-906821-70-8

Brand and product names are trademarks or registered trademarks
of their respective owners.

Cover designed by D.R.ink
Typeset by Nicki Averill
Printed and bound in the UK by CPI Antony Rowe,
Chippenham and Eastbourne

FOR GEORGE AND ANNIE

FIFE COUNCIL LIBRARIES	
EC FB050957	
DONATION	2/12/12
JR	—
JF	CP

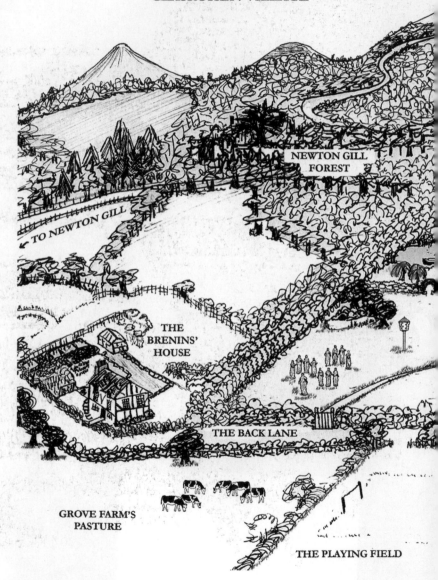

THE MAP
OF
GLASRUHEN VILLAGE

NEWTON GILL FOREST

← TO NEWTON GILL

THE BRENINS' HOUSE

THE BACK LANE

GROVE FARM'S PASTURE

THE PLAYING FIELD

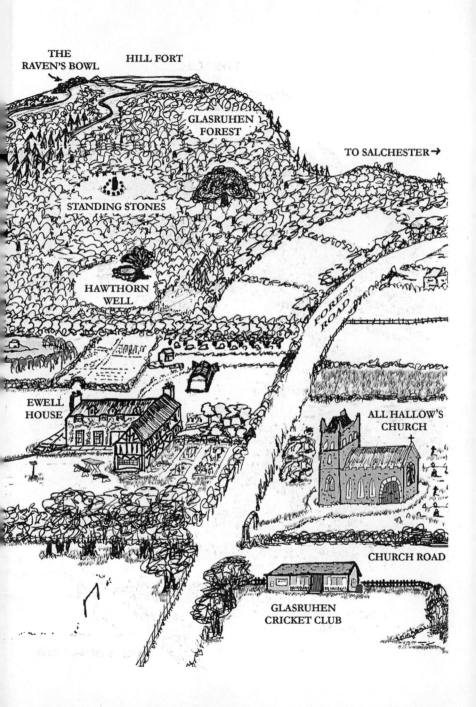

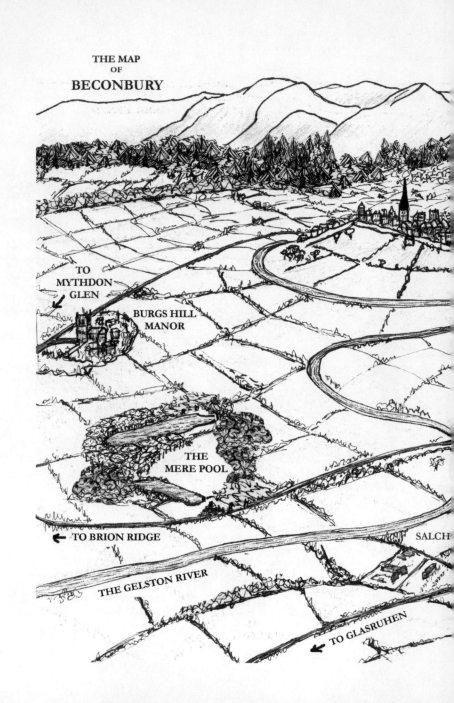

THE MAP
OF
BECONBURY

TO
MYTHDON
GLEN

BURGS HILL
MANOR

THE
MERE POOL

← TO BRION RIDGE

SALCH

THE GELSTON RIVER

TO GLASRUHEN

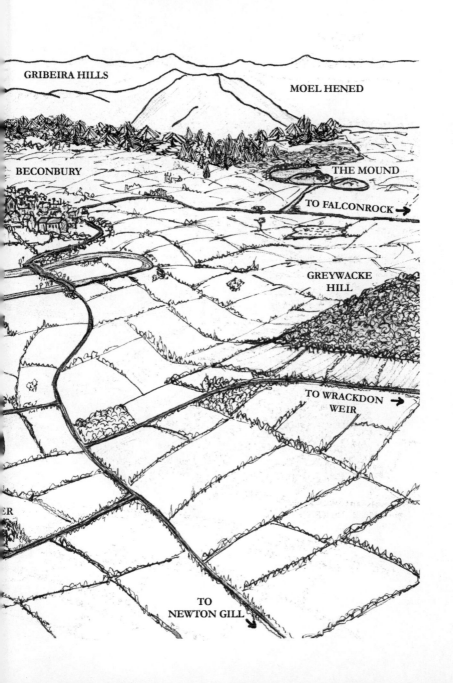

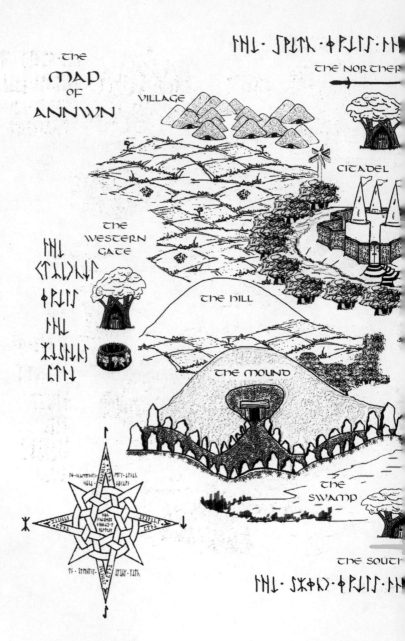

THE · ᛋᛈᛠᛏᚻ · ᚩᚱᛈᛁᛋ · ᚻᚻ
THE NORTHER

THE
MAP
OF
ANNWN

VILLAGE

CITADEL

THE
WESTERN
GATE

ᚻᚻᛁ
ᚳᛏᛋᛁᛈᚻᛈᛋ
ᚩᚱᛈᛁᛋ
ᚻᚻᛁ
ᚷᛁᛋᚻᛈᛋ
ᚳᛏᚻᛁ

THE HILL

THE MOUND

THE
SWAMP

THE SOUTH

THE · ᛋᚷᚩᚻᛈ · ᚩᚱᛈᛁᛋ · ᚻᚻ

ᚠᚪᚱᚻᛁᛚᚱ · ᚷᛏᚪᛁ

SILYTYYY

THE DRUIDS
VILLAGE

THE
MOUNTAINS

THE · ᚷᛏᚣᛚᛋ · ᚩᚠ
ᛁᛁᛚᚪᛁᛏᛁ · ᚻᛁᛋᚠ
ᛏᛁᛁ · ᛁᚠ · THE
Mᚩᚢᛁᛏᛁᛁᛋ

THE
THER
AK

THE
GLASS
PALACE

THE
CLEARING

THE
EASTERN
GATE

THE MONOLITH

THE
Sᚻᚩᛏᛁ · ᚩᚠ
ᚦᛁᛋᚻᚠᚣ
ᚩᛈᛁᛋᛋ
THE
ᛁᛏᛋᛁᛚᛁᛋ
ᚷᛏᚪᛁ

THE AMPITHEATRE

THE
CAUSEWAY

THE
CRANNOG

N GATE

ᛋᚩᚪᚻᚻᛁᛚᚱ · ᚷᛏᚪᛁᚴ

THE PROPHECY

A Brenin boy you'll need to find
Born at Samhain of Humankind.
The One you seek is brave and strong
And his true heart will do no wrong.
The Golden Acorn he will see
And listen to the Dryad's plea.
Underneath Glasruhen Hill
He'll make a promise he'll fulfil.
When all is equal, all the same
That which was lost is found again.

WHEN ALL IS EQUAL ALL THE SAME

THAT WHICH WAS LOST IS FOUND AGAIN

CONTENTS

WHEN THEY'RE FOUND AND BROUGHT TOGETHER.

BIND THEM UP WITH THONGS OF LEATHER.

PROLOGUE

'We're back,' croaked Camelin as he flew over the tall hedge that surrounded Ewell House.

Jack wasn't far behind. He could see Motley and the Night Guard scurrying towards the kitchen door as he too flew over the hedge. Gerda hurried onto the patio and two small bats flitted around the doorway.

'We're back, we did it!' Camelin announced to everyone who'd come to welcome them.

'Where's Orin?' Jack shouted to Motley as he made his descent.

'Up here!' an excited, squeaky voice replied from the open window of Camelin's loft.

Jack saw Camelin land on the grass and proudly strut towards the waiting group. Seconds later, he too had landed. Orin appeared at the kitchen door and rushed over to them. Timmery and Charkle fluttered around their heads. Everyone was asking questions at once. Camelin flew onto the picnic table and swaggered up and down, and then he threw back his head and loudly made the call of the *raven-owl*. Everything went quiet as they waited for him to speak. He puffed out his chest feathers, cocked his head to one side and slowly looked at each face. Jack could see the rats were desperate to hear what Camelin had to say.

'We'll tell you everything, but not until after we've had breakfast. I'm starving.'

There was a groan of disappointment and then they all turned to Jack.

'I'm starving too.'

'We'd better eat then,' Nora announced as she and Elan joined the group.

Gerda cackled loudly then stopped abruptly and turned towards the lake. Another goose could be heard in the distance.

'You have a visitor,' Elan explained.

Jack smiled. Gerda was going to be one very happy goose when she got to the lake and found Medric waiting for her. They all watched as she hurried away.

'A visitor,' piped Timmery. 'Oh I love visitors.'

Camelin humphed but no one seemed to notice. All the rats were looking at Nora.

'You'll find out who it is soon enough. Shall we go and eat now?'

'Great!' croaked Camelin taking off and swooping into the kitchen.

There was a scampering and a flittering and soon only Nora and Jack were left on the patio.

'I'm going to need to know everything. And I mean everything.'

Jack nodded. He knew they'd have to tell Nora about the Roman soldiers, what they had done to Camelin, and about their narrow escape from Viroconium. She'd find out eventually, even if they didn't tell her. There was a rustling of leaves from the hedge. Jack watched as a message made its way from the great yews to the trees beyond. Soon it would be in the depths of Glasruhen Forest.

'When can we go and see Arrana?'

'After breakfast. We'll go there first and collect the three cauldron plates the Dryads have been guarding. Then we'll go and see Jennet and get back the ones you found.'

'Could I transform first? I'm feeling all squashed.'

'Of course you can. Fly to the loft and I'll send Camelin up. He'll just have to wait a bit longer for his breakfast.'

Jack hopped in through the loft window. The two raven baskets were in the centre of the room. His clothes were in a pile by the beanbag where he'd left them. It felt as if he'd been away for weeks rather than hours. He was so pleased to be back. His thoughts were interrupted by Camelin's arrival.

'Come on, let's get on with it. I'm hungry.'

They touched foreheads. Even with his eyes tightly closed the blinding light still hurt. When Jack could see again Camelin was already perched on the windowsill.

'You will hurry up won't you? Nora says we can't start without you.'

Jack dressed as quickly as he could and then dashed down the stairs and along the corridor. When he entered the kitchen everyone clapped and cheered. Jack felt his cheeks burning as he made his way to the only empty chair. Camelin's voice croaked above the noise: 'Can we start now?'

RECOVERY

Jack let Camelin tell everyone about their journey into the past, adding bits here and there whenever Camelin missed anything out. Jack could see that Nora didn't look pleased. It was obvious that Camelin was enjoying being the centre of attention and if he'd seen the looks Nora was giving him, he'd chosen to ignore them. There'd been a lot of questions, especially about Medric, so it had taken a long time to get to the end.

'And then we had breakfast,' Camelin said as he bowed.

The rats cheered. Orin scrambled up to sit on Jack's shoulder and rubbed her soft fur against his cheek.

'Again, again,' piped Timmery flitting around Camelin's head. 'Tell us the bit about Jennet again.'

Camelin took a deep breath.

'Jack put the three cauldron plates into Jennet's hand. She didn't like the look of them and dropped them in the spring. Then she saw the Camp Prefect in all his shiny armour. She got really excited. One minute he's there, the next he's gone. Then he's back again, all dripping wet and dressed only in his tunic. You should have seen his face after Jennet stripped him of every bit of shiny metal he possessed. He was shaking all over.'

They all laughed, except Nora.

'You promised you'd come straight back through the window in time if you were in any danger. I thought you always kept your promises Jack.'

'I do. But I also promised to help find the missing cauldron plates.'

'You should have left the plates.'

'How could I when so much depends on you remaking the cauldron?'

'If I'd known you were going to end up in Viroconium I'd never have asked you to go in the first place.'

Camelin pulled a face.

'The prophecy said we'd succeed, remember? *That*

which was lost is found again. Jack's *The One.* You said so yourself.'

'But you could have been hurt.'

No one spoke. Jack thought he'd better try to change the subject.

'Can we go and see Arrana soon?'

'We can, but there's something we have to do before we go into Glasruhen,' Nora replied. 'We need to lay the cauldron plates out in order so I can lace them all together when we bring the others back.'

She led the way out of the kitchen to the herborium.

'This won't take long, and then we'll go to collect the three plates from Arrana. On the way back we'll make an exchange with Jennet for the ones Jack gave her.'

Jack searched his pockets.

'I haven't got anything to give Jennet for the exchange.'

Elan laughed and pulled a small bottle out of her pocket before handing it to Jack.

'Don't worry. We've given this a great deal of thought. I don't think she'll be able to resist this.'

Jack examined the bottle.

'It's nail varnish!'

'It's very special nail varnish, look.'

Elan wriggled her fingers. The varnish was dark green, about the same colour as Jennet's hair. Her nails shone and sparkled as tiny specks of glitter caught the light.

'Oh wow! She'll love that.'

'Here we are,' Nora announced when they were all gathered around the long table in the middle of the herborium.

At one end Jack could see a pile of leather thongs. At the other end was a pile of cauldron plates similar to the ones he'd had in his hands only hours before.

Nora took a book from the shelf and flicked through the pages until she found what she was looking for. Jack felt excited. He realised it wouldn't be long before he'd see the whole cauldron. Elan put the large round base plate, embossed with the yew tree, in the centre of the table.

Nora offered the book to Jack.

'Maybe you could read this while Elan and I arrange the plates we've got.'

The book was heavy, and like all the other books at Ewell House it was handmade. The page he was looking at was beautifully decorated and showed all thirteen plates laid out around the circular base plate. He read each name in order, starting at number one, which was the pine.

Nora and Elan sorted through the six plates and laid them around the base as Jack read their names. They left spaces for the ones they hadn't got. When they'd finished Nora smiled.

'I'd almost given up hope of ever seeing the cauldron whole again. We're going to be able to use it for the feast at Samhain now. Shall we go?'

Without waiting for an answer, Nora strode out of the door and made her way to the bottom of the garden. Jack and Elan followed, while Camelin flew on ahead.

Jack had first gone into Glasruhen Forest only a few weeks ago, but it felt like he'd known it for years. He watched the now familiar sight of Nora standing before the blackthorn hedge. As her hands came together she raised them in a circular motion. This time, when the hedge parted, Jack's knees didn't tremble. He was eager to speak to Arrana. Desperate for her to know that he'd kept his promise and succeeded. Now the forest would be saved. Once the cauldron was remade, they could go into Annwn. Nora could collect acorns from the Mother Oak for Arrana and leaves from the Crochan tree for the elixir. Arrana could pass on her knowledge and a new Hamadryad would take her place in the sacred grove. Nora would be fine once she'd drunk the elixir again.

Jack stepped into the tunnel. There was rustling. Without looking back he knew that the hedge had sealed itself.

'Don't be long,' Camelin croaked as he flew overhead before disappearing out of sight.

The dense yews blocked out the sunlight and made the forest look gloomy. It was stuffy inside the tunnel but the swaying branches created a slight breeze. Needle-like leaves brushed Jack's shoulders. Was it his imagination or were the great yews reaching out to touch him? He was so deep in thought that he didn't see Elan stop and he nearly bumped into her.

'Something's wrong,' she whispered.

'What is it?'

'Over there. Look.'

In the distance Jack could see a group of Dryads. They were swaying from side to side. When he got closer Jack could see that they didn't look happy. The nearest nymph stepped forward and bowed her head before speaking to Nora.

'Oh Great Seanchai, Keeper of Secrets and Guardian of the Sacred Grove, we cannot deliver our messages. Arrana the Wise, Protector and Most Sacred of All will not awaken.'

'This isn't good news,' Nora muttered.

The Dryads clung to each other.

'It took us ages to wake her up the last time Camelin and I came to see her,' said Jack.

The tallest Dryad stepped forward.

'We've already tried singing to her.'

Nora looked worried.

'I don't think we have much time. As Arrana fades my magic will weaken too. We must hurry.'

The Dryads moved quickly, it was impossible to keep up with them and they were soon out of sight. As they neared the centre of the forest they heard a low mournful sound.

'Hurry,' urged Nora.

They came to an abrupt halt in the clearing. The sound was coming from the Dryads who had surrounded Arrana. Worried faces turned towards them but they didn't stop their sorrowful song. The circle parted to let Nora through, Jack and Elan followed. Camelin flew down to join them.

'Shall I sing?'

'No Camelin, I don't think that's going to help,' replied Nora kindly. She stood in front of the great Hamadryad and raised her head.

'Arrana, The Wise, Lady of the Wood and Most Sacred of All, we have good news for you.'

The forest was silent. Every face turned towards Arrana. Nora tried again but the great oak didn't stir so she took out her wand.

'I was hoping I wouldn't have to use this,' she muttered to herself. 'Come help me Jack. Take the golden acorn and hold it in your palm. When it begins to glow, try to direct the light towards Arrana.'

Jack opened his hand. The golden acorn felt warm and heavy. Tiny red sparks spluttered from the tip of Nora's glowing wand.

'*Deffro hun,*' she commanded.

A shaft of golden light burst from the acorn. He heard a gasp from the Dryads. His hand trembled as he tried to control the light. Nora raised her wand and pointed it directly at the Hamadryad's branches. Again, she repeated the words.

'*Deffro hun.*'

A green flash from the wand lit the grove. A slight movement from Arrana's trunk made them all hold their breath.

'*Deffro hun*,' repeated Nora.

This time the trunk began to waver. It shimmered and shook as it gained momentum, until at last, Arrana stood before them. As she shook her hair, leaves cascaded to the ground. They all bowed.

Jack could see the concern in Nora's eyes. Arrana looked so thin you could see right through her. Almost all of her leaves had fallen. Her long hair looked thinner too. When she spoke her voice sounded weary.

'You have news?'

'We do,' Nora replied. 'That which was lost has been found again. We are ready to remake the cauldron.'

There was rustling and whispering. The Dryads and trees all seemed to be talking at once. Arrana listened to what they had to say before turning to Jack.

'You did well Jack Brenin. Come nearer.'

Jack obeyed.

'We are all very grateful to you for finding the lost cauldron plates. Because of your courage the forests will be saved. I still have strength enough to grant you a reward.'

Jack bowed low to Arrana before speaking.

'I don't need a reward. I wanted to help.'

He could feel the colour rising in his cheeks. He didn't want to take all the credit.

'I couldn't have done it without Camelin.'

'And he couldn't have completed the quest without you. You may ask for anything that it is within my power to grant.'

Jack shook his head. He really had been glad to help. It wouldn't be right to take something for himself.

'Could I ask for something for someone else?'

'You may.'

'Could you give Camelin a lath?'

Everyone looked at Jack. Camelin's beak fell open and his eyes grew as big as saucers.

'It would be my pleasure, but what use would a lath be to an acolyte who never finished his training? Camelin may have his lath when he can read and write.'

Jack smiled as Camelin shuffled in front of Nora. He picked up a stick in his beak and wrote his name in the soft loam.

'Camelin,' he read, and then puffed out his feathers.

Arrana looked at Nora.

'Jack's been teaching him to read but I didn't know he could write as well.'

'Your wish is granted Jack.'

Arrana turned to Camelin.

'Take this twig and use it well. A part of Annwn will always be with you.'

Camelin took the gnarled twig from Arrana and bowed low.

'Thank you,' said Jack.

'Now is that all? I grow weary. You have many things to do and so little time.'

'We need the plates you've been keeping safe,' said Elan.

'Oh yes. The plates.'

Arrana turned her head slowly and pointed towards a tall willowy Dryad with pale green skin and long chestnut hair.

'Cory will show you where the plates have been hidden. I need to rest now.'

Arrana sighed deeply as her bark began to shimmer and shake. When she had disappeared they stood in silence before the gnarled trunk of the ancient oak until Cory stepped forward.

'Will you follow me?'

She quickly led them across the hillside. They had to hurry to keep up with her.

'We're here,' she announced when they were standing before a group of bushes with strange twisted branches. They were so thick it was impossible to see anything through them.

Cory stepped into the first bush and disappeared. Jack wondered if they were expected to do the same but no one made any move to follow. Two more Dryads appeared and touched the leaves of the bush Cory had entered. The branches swished from side to side until an opening appeared.

'Come through,' Cory said from the other side.

They stepped into a circular clearing. A large stone stood in the centre, and there were smaller ones around the edge.

'This place is protected by the deepest magic. None may enter without Arrana's permission,' Cory explained as she led them towards the centre.

Jack could see the stones had been carved with strange markings. They were different from the ones he'd seen around Jennet's well. These were more like lines, scratched deeply into the stone. The tallest stone had a hole through the middle. Cory put her hands inside the hole and spoke to the stone. There was a loud crack as the ground split open at its base. She bent down and removed something large that was wrapped in cloth. Then the ground closed again.

'I believe these are what you need?' she said as she

offered Nora the bundle.

'Thank you, Cory. Please thank the trees for looking after my plates so well. Soon the cauldron will be remade and we'll make all speed into Annwn to collect the acorns. We will have Hamadryads in the forests again to protect you all.'

Cory bowed and signalled for them to go back through the strange bush. Once they were in the forest Nora opened the package and spread the plates out on the ground.

'That's the rowan, ash and birch. Only three more to collect. Shall we go and see Jennet now?'

As they made their way to the Hawthorn Well, Camelin hopped and skipped around the meadow with his lath held firmly in his beak.

'Thanks Jack. I can't believe I've got a wand at last.'

'It's alright. You deserve it.'

Nora frowned at Camelin.

'When you've empowered it you'd better join Jack for wand practice. I don't want you misusing it.'

They walked the rest of the way through the meadow in silence, lost in their own thoughts. Even though he should have felt elated Jack couldn't stop thinking about Arrana.

Nora had already got her lips to the water and was calling Jennet's name by the time Jack and Elan arrived at the well. They watched as the water began to bubble. A column of water rose. Green matted hair appeared, followed by a very cross-looking water nymph.

'It's not two minutes since you were here last. What now?'

'Jack has something to ask you,' said Nora.

Jack stepped forward and shuffled his feet as Jennet sniffed the air impatiently.

'Come on, come on, I haven't got all day.'

'I've come to collect the cauldron plates.'

'And if I've got any, what do I get in return? Cauldron plates are very precious. Not many about these days.'

Elan stepped forward.

'We have some very powerful magic. It can make you look even more beautiful than you already are.'

Jack could see Jennet was interested. Elan showed her the bottle.

'The magic is inside.'

Jennet thrust her head forward and peered at the glass.

'What kind of magic?'

'Green magic.'

Camelin chuckled and Jack tried his best not to laugh.

'Show me,' crooned Jennet.

Elan opened the bottle. The powerful smell of the nail varnish filled the air. Jennet sniffed then put her tongue out and tasted the pungent aroma.

'That's powerful magic indeed. How does it work?'

Elan wriggled her fingernails then demonstrated the magic by painting one of Jennet's nails.

'Oh most acceptable. I'll go and find you some plates.'

They all laughed after Jennet had disappeared into the well. They could hear crashing and banging coming from deep under the water. Occasionally bubbles rose to the surface. Finally Jennet reappeared with a whole collection of old cauldron plates. Nora didn't look happy.

'These are not the right ones Jennet. Jack gave you three plates, and all of them had trees embossed on them. Don't you remember? One of them used to hang next to the well, it had a hawthorn tree on it. The other two are similar. One has the oak, the other a willow.'

'This is all I've got. I've gone through my whole collection down there. If I'd had the well plate I'd have put it back a long time ago. Besides, Jack never gave me any plates to look after.'

'I did, I gave them to you and you threw them into the spring.'

'Spring?'

'The one at Viroconium.'

'Wasn't me. Now I'll just be taking my bottle and be off. I've got lots to do today.'

Nora unwrapped the bundle she was carrying.

'Take a look Jennet, they're like these.'

'Nothing like them down below. Come and look if you don't believe me.'

'Could you just go and take one more look?' Jack pleaded.

'I know what I've got in my cupboards Jack Brenin and what's more, I know you never gave me any cauldron plates. I would remember.'

The water began to gurgle and boil and Jennet abruptly disappeared.

'I'm sure it was Jennet. You thought it was her too, didn't you Camelin?'

'It was dark, could have been any water nymph, they're all bad tempered. Seen one, seen 'em all.'

'What happens now?' Jack asked Nora.

'She'll be back. She'll want the bottle now she's seen it.'

'How long will we have to wait? You said we were running out of time. We need to get the plates back as soon as possible, don't we?'

PROBLEMS

'What about my symbol?' asked Camelin as he looked around the base of Jennet's well.

'I'm afraid that's going to have to wait. Recovering the plates is far more important,' Nora told him.

Camelin frowned.

'But I've waited a long time for a lath.'

'Waiting a little longer isn't going to make much difference is it?'

Camelin sighed deeply.

'Couldn't you just…'

'No and that's an end to the matter. You'll get your mark eventually.'

Jack paced up and down in front of the well.

'Do you think she's forgotten about the plates?'

'Water nymphs can be forgetful,' said Elan. 'It might help if you remind her what happened, when she comes up again.'

'She will come up again, won't she?'

Before Elan could reply the water in the well began to bubble. Nora stood by the water's edge and was ready as soon as Jennet reappeared.

'I don't believe we finished our conversation, did we? Jack has something he'd like to ask you.'

'I've already told you. There aren't any more cauldron plates.'

'Do you have any armour?' asked Jack.

'Armour! What would I be doing with armour?'

'The Camp Prefect at Viroconium had lots of shiny armour and weapons. I just thought they were the sort of thing a water nymph might have taken a fancy to.'

'Some might, but not me. I stayed right away from Romans.'

'Did you ever go to Viroconium?'

'Never.'

Jack sighed. He was getting nowhere. Elan put her hand on Jack's shoulder and stepped forward.

'Who would have been in the spring at Viroconium?'

'How would I know? What did she look like?'

'She looked very much like you,' said Jack nervously.

Jennet ran her long green fingers down her cheeks before thrusting her head towards Jack.

'Was she as beautiful?'

Jack was going to say it was dark and he hadn't seen her too well, but Camelin interrupted before he could speak.

'Nowhere near as beautiful as you and her hair was a lot greener than yours.'

'Hmm, not as beautiful, darker hair, a few hundred years ago, Viroconium. Don't go away, I'll be right back.'

'Do you think she knows who it was?' asked Jack.

'I think I know what she's gone to fetch,' replied Nora. 'Jennet likes to be well informed, so she has a list of all the water nymphs. Just in case any of them might be more beautiful than she is!'

'Here we are,' Jennet announced as she resurfaced. 'My list.'

She had three slates in her hand. Jack could see that the top one had strange markings scratched onto it. They were like the ones they'd seen on the standing stone earlier. Jennet coughed then began reading the names:

'Isen, Nymet, Myryl, Kerrin, Coriss, Uriel, Lucie…'

'How many names are on the list?' Elan asked.

'Too many,' grumbled Camelin.

Nora gave him a disapproving look then smiled at Jennet.

'Could you find out quickly for us which nymph it might have been?'

'Don't do information, you need a Bogie for that,' Jennet replied, thrusting the slates into Nora's hand before disappearing, once more, into the well.

'It looks like we're going to have to pay Peabody a visit. I'd hoped we wouldn't have to see him again so soon.'

'You didn't ask her for my sign?' grumbled Camelin.

'And she didn't ask for the…' began Elan, just before a surge of bubbles exploded from the well.

'My green magic…' crooned Jennet as she stretched out her long fingers towards Elan.

'My symbol,' demanded Camelin.

'A symbol? Now what would you be wanting with one of those?'

'Camelin has a lath now,' explained Jack.

Jennet looked surprised.

'And in return for the symbol I can have the magic bottle?'

'Yes,' agreed Nora.

Jennet leant over the rim of the well and sniffed the air.

'Here it is. Come and touch it.'

Camelin shuffled over and touched the rock with the end of his beak. There was a sudden flash. A symbol, carved deeply into the rock, began to glow. The tip of Camelin's beak glowed too.

'Hot, hot!' Camelin shouted as he hopped around.

Sparks flew out of the end of Camelin's wand. One landed on top of Jack's head followed by the smell of burning hair.

'I'm burning!' yelled Jack.

Nora scooped up a handful of water and threw it over Jack's head.

'You said I was dangerous with my wand! Look what you've done with yours, you've singed my hair.'

'Now, now, you two,' chided Nora. 'It was an accident. Your hair will grow back Jack. It's only made a small bald patch.'

'Can't we grow it back with magic?' asked Jack.

'I haven't got a lot of magic to spare at the moment. I'm saving what little I've got left for when we need it. Besides, growing hair with magic isn't advisable, you never know what might happen. It could come back pink. It's better to let it grow back naturally.'

Camelin chuckled. There was a strange rasping noise coming from the well as Jennet laughed too. She wriggled her fingers impatiently. As soon as Elan put the bottle in her hand she vanished.

'Well, we seem to have a problem,' sighed Nora. 'I hadn't anticipated this. I'd hoped we could remake the cauldron again this afternoon.'

Elan looked at the slates.

'We're going to have to find Peabody. We haven't got time to visit all the nymphs on Jennet's list.'

'We'll go,' volunteered Jack, smiling at Camelin.

'We will?'

'It'd be quicker if you flew,' said Elan.

'We'll take your clothes and wands. Come back to the house as soon as you've got the information we need from Peabody,' said Nora. 'With any luck you won't have to search far, he might still be in the Gnori in Newton Gill Forest.'

Jack and Camelin transformed and flew off towards Newton Gill.

They landed on one of the Gnarles lower branches.

'Hello,' Jack shouted.

'Hello to you,' replied a sleepy voice from the tree they were perched in.

'Have you seen Peabody?' Jack asked. 'He's the Bogie you saved me from the last time I was here.'

'I've got a good memory for faces, but I don't remember speaking to any ravens lately.'

'It's Jack. Jack Brenin.'

The Gnarle screwed up his eyes and peered up at Jack.

'He's a raven boy now, like me,' explained Camelin.

'A raven boy, why didn't you say? Have you come to sing to us again Jack. You did promise.'

'We're in a bit of a hurry at the moment. We need to see Peabody. Is he still living in the Gnori?'

'Oh yes, he's still there. He's had it all done up

since you were here last. Got a new front door. Lots of comings and goings. Getting busy again in the forest but no one ever gives us a second glance. It'd be nice to hear a song again, now you're here.'

'Well, maybe one verse, but then we really will have to go.'

'What about the one that starts again at the end?' said Camelin. 'You know the one I mean, don't you? It's about an old man and the whiskers on his chin. I like that one, it goes on forever.'

Jack nodded. He knew the song Camelin wanted to sing.

They swooped down to the forest floor and began croaking loudly:

There once was a man named Michael Finnegan,
He grew whiskers on his chinnegan,
The wind came up and blew them in ag'in,
Poor old Michael Finnegan (begin ag'in).

The Gnarle stopped them.

'That's quite all right; you don't need to *begin again*. Didn't you say you were in a hurry? Maybe when you've got a bit more time, and you're a boy again, you could come back and sing to us?'

'I will,' Jack promised as he and Camelin set off towards the Gnori.

The Gnarle had been right. Instead of an open crack in the hollow trunk of the old oak, Jack could see a brand new front door. A large notice written in crooked capital letters had been pinned to it.

'NOT AT HOME,' read Camelin before rapping on the door with his beak.

'Can't you read?' shouted an angry voice from inside. 'I'm not at home.'

'I can read and you obviously *are* at home.'

'Not to visitors I'm not.'

'This is important. We've come on an errand from Nora,' Jack croaked.

There were a lot of hurrying footsteps followed by bolts being drawn. Finally, a key turned in the lock and the door opened slightly. A long nose appeared through the crack.

'From the Great Seanchai, you say?'

'Hurry up and let us in. This is important,' grumbled Camelin.

'She needs your help,' explained Jack.

'My help! Why didn't you say so in the first place? Come in, come in. Go straight through. Just follow the tunnel.'

The door slammed and was locked behind them.

'Here we are,' Peabody announced as they entered a large room.

Some of the roots from the hollow tree above were poking through the walls and an array of hats hung on them. There was a collection of coins and shiny things on the table which Peabody hurriedly covered with a cloth.

'It reminds me of a Spriggan's tunnel,' said Jack as he looked at the smooth walls.

'That's probably because Spriggans made it. A sort of compensation for my brother getting me into so much trouble.'

Peabody stroked his long nose before speaking again.

'Now, how can I be of service?'

'We need to know which water nymph would have been in the spring at Viroconium,' explained Jack.

Peabody rubbed his chin.

'That's a long time ago. I'm going to need my thinking hat for that one.'

'Thinking hat? I thought most people had a thinking *cap*!' said Jack trying not to laugh.

'That's *most people*. Now let me see, which one goes back a few hundred years?'

Peabody paced up and down in front of the row of hats before choosing the most battered one.

'It used to have a beautiful feather stuck in the band. I don't suppose either of you have got a feather to spare?'

'No we have not,' snapped Camelin. 'Now, if you don't mind, can you come up with an answer? We don't have much time.'

Peabody put the hat on, sat down on a tree stump and closed his eyes.

'Viroconium you say?'

'Viroconium,' Jack and Camelin confirmed together.

Peabody sat and muttered to himself for what seemed like a very long time. At last he stood up and replaced the hat.

'Well?' said Camelin expectantly.

'I've gone through every water nymph I can think of. I only know of three who've ever lived west of here. It's going to be Coriss, Myryl or Uriel. They're Undines, they prefer wells and springs.'

'Oh great!' Camelin grumbled. 'Three of them.'

'Well it's better than having to go through all the names on Jennet's list,' whispered Jack.

'I hope I've been of help. You will tell the Great Seanchai how helpful I've been, won't you?'

'We will, but we'd better be going now. Thank you,' said Jack.

Peabody led the way back to his new front door and let them out. As soon as the door shut behind them the key was turned and the bolts were slid noisily back.

'You did well,' Nora said when they told her about their meeting with Peabody. 'Go and transform now and we'll all give this a bit of thought.'

'Have you met any of the nymphs before?' Jack asked Camelin as he dressed.

'Only Myryl, but it was a long time ago now. Come on! Race you downstairs.'

It wasn't much of a race. Camelin flew while Jack had to take the stairs. By the time he got to the kitchen Elan and Nora were already discussing the nymphs on Peabody's list.

'Isn't Myryl an expert on cauldrons?' asked Elan.

'You're right. She'd be the best one to start with, she knows just about everything there is to know about cauldrons. We'll visit her first, but not until tomorrow.

It's getting late. Jack, you ought to be getting back home. You've had a very busy weekend and it's school tomorrow.'

'But I wanted to go with you.'

'We can't go without you,' replied Elan.

Nora agreed.

'If you've given a water nymph something and you need it back, you have to ask for it yourself. You also need to have something ready for the exchange, and it has to something special.'

'What will I give her for the plates? Do you think she'd like some nail varnish too?'

Nora shook her head.

'From what I remember of Myryl she likes big things, she's a lot more sociable than Jennet, she likes to talk...'

'And talk and talk,' interrupted Camelin. 'She's as bad as Timmery.'

'Isn't that good, at least she'll tell us what she knows, won't she?' asked Jack.

'It would be, if she could keep her mind on one thing at a time, but she sort of flits from one thing to another. She gets back to the reason you've called eventually, but it can take a long time.'

'At least she doesn't mind visitors,' continued Nora.

'I said she was like Timmery,' Camelin grumbled to himself.

'So what am I going to give her?'

'It will take a bit of thought, but I'm sure we'll come up with something.'

'If Myryl is an expert on cauldrons we'll need to offer her something similar,' said Elan, thinking aloud.

'How about one of those Hallowe'en buckets you can buy? The ones you take round for trick-or-treating to put all your sweets in,' suggested Jack. 'We could spray it silver.'

Camelin's head shot up and he hopped over to Jack.

'People give you sweets in a bucket? Have you got one of those buckets? When can we go? We can't give it to Myryl if it's for sweets!'

'We certainly can't,' replied Nora. 'I know the ones you mean Jack. They're the right shape but the wrong material. They're usually black plastic. We need something shiny and metallic. I think the paint would wear off quite quickly under water.'

'A saucepan then, a big one with two handles like they have in the kitchen at school,' continued Jack.

'That's a possibility,' replied Nora. 'But I still don't think it would be big enough.'

'How big are those buckets?' Camelin asked Jack, 'The ones you collect the sweets in?'

Jack made a shape with his hands.

'About the same size as a football.'

'That's not very big, couldn't we use a dustbin? We'd get a lot more sweets in one of them.'

'That's a brilliant idea!' exclaimed Nora.

Camelin's beak fell open.

'Do you mean it? You're going to get a dustbin?'

'A dustbin would be perfect,' agreed Elan. 'But not one of those new plastic ones, we need an old-fashioned ribbed galvanised bin.'

Jack could see what an amazing exchange a bright new shiny galvanised dustbin would be.

Camelin looked excited. He was hopping from one foot to the other.

'When can we go and get the sweets?'

'What sweets?' they all asked.

'The ones to go in my dustbin!'

'The dustbin's for Myryl; haven't you been listening?' Nora asked. 'I'll go down into the village first thing in the morning and buy one. Then I'll call in and see your grandad and tell him we're off on an outing and you're invited to come along. We'll pick you up straight after school and make our way over to see Myryl.'

'Is it far?' asked Jack.

Elan got Nora's map down from the dresser and spread it out on the table.

'She lives somewhere around here, in a spring above one of the lakes near the Welsh border. There used to be lots of lakes in that area. People built forts there on the mounds, but that was a long time ago. There's not much water left now.'

Jack looked over at Camelin. He'd not been looking at the map.

'What's wrong?' he asked.

'Nothing.'

Nora laughed.

'He'll be fine, once he gets over the loss of a dustbin full of sweets he never had!'

From his bedroom window Jack watched the sky darken. A storm was rumbling in the distance. He'd expected Grandad to ask him about his weekend but instead he'd told Jack all about the gardening club and what he was going to enter in this year's competition.

Jack was relieved he hadn't had to say anything about what he'd done. He couldn't tell Grandad the truth, he couldn't tell anyone. They'd think he was crazy, especially if he said he'd gone back in time to Roman Britain.

By bedtime rain was lashing at the windows. Jack wished Camelin was there to talk to, he missed his company, but it was unlikely he'd leave his dry loft on a night like this. A loud clap of thunder rumbled overhead. Orin climbed up onto the windowsill to watch the storm with Jack. She jumped each time lightning flashed across the sky and shook as the thunder exploded. The rain made a deafening noise as it beat against the window.

'Don't worry, it can't hurt you,' he told her as he held his arm out so she could climb up to sit on his shoulder. 'I hope it's a better day tomorrow when we go to see Myryl.'

Jack was just about to get into bed when his Book of Shadows vibrated.

Elan must have sent him a message. He opened it at the first page and watched as the message appeared. When he saw what it said he smiled. It wasn't from Elan.

I hav my own buk to writ in
we can writ tonit so I wont get wet

Jack laughed. Camelin might have learnt to read but he needed a lot of practice with his spelling. He wrote back:

I'll see you in the morning.

He didn't have to wait long for an answer:

how many swets do u think I cud get in a dustbin

Jack laughed and replied:

It would depend on the size of the bin.

There were no more messages. Jack lay in bed but couldn't sleep. He wondered if Camelin was dreaming about dustbins overflowing with sweets. He'd thought it would be easy to retrieve the plates once they'd come back through the window in time. Tonight they should have been celebrating and making plans to go into Annwn. Jack couldn't help worrying. How was he going to get through a whole day at school? He wondered what would happen when they found Myryl. She had to have the plates. Didn't she?

MYRYL

'Over here Jack,' Elan shouted as she waved from the end of the road.

Jack made his way as quickly as he could towards her through the other children and parents congregated outside the school gates.

'That was a long day. I thought it was never going to end. Have you got everything we need?'

'We're ready to go. Nora's parked just around the corner.'

Jack got into the back of the car and looked over the seat. A large shiny dustbin had been laid on its side. A long, cloth-wrapped object was beside it. Jack presumed it was one of the cauldron plates.

'Where's Camelin?'

'In here,' came a muffled reply from inside the dustbin.

'What are you doing in there?'

'Nora made me get in. I'm supposed to be inconspicuous, whatever that means. I can tell you what I am though. I'm very uncomfortable.'

Nora laughed.

'You won't be in there for long. As soon as we leave Newton Gill you can come out. I've put a pair of Elan's old wellingtons in the car for you Jack. I think it's going to be a bit muddy by the spring after all the rain we had last night.'

'Thanks. Will it take long to get there?'

Elan passed a road map over to Jack.

'We're heading north west. It should take about half an hour, but we don't know exactly which spring Myryl's going to be in. Camelin can scout around when we get there.'

'Can I come out it's stuffy in here?'

'Yes, I think it's safe now,' said Nora.

In all the excitement Jack had forgotten to tell Camelin his news.

'I made the choir. We start rehearsals for the end of term concert next week. I've been asked to sing a solo too.'

They all congratulated him.

Jack woke with a start. He must have fallen asleep.

'You've been snoring,' said Camelin.

'Sorry. I didn't sleep much last night and it's hot in the car.'

'You haven't missed much.'

'We're almost there,' Nora informed them. 'You'll need to go and have a good look around Camelin. Try the obvious places first. She's bound to be somewhere quiet. She likes visitors, but not crowds of people.'

Nora stopped the car by a field. She opened the door and Camelin flew off towards a small mound in the centre that was covered in trees.

'This whole area used to be under water, apart from those two mounds,' Elan told Jack as she pointed in the direction Camelin had gone. 'They used to be joined by a raised causeway. The Cornovii lived here, part of the same people who used to live on Glasruhen. It was abandoned round about the time the Romans invaded the area.'

Jack looked at the small hillock.

'It doesn't look anything like a hillfort. It should have been called a moundfort.'

Nora sighed.

'It used to be a magnificent sight. You could see the raised embankment and round dwellings reflected in the water. All that's left now is one small lake. You'd never know that people once lived here.'

'What's Myrel like?' asked Jack.

'She looks like Jennet. Most water nymphs are pretty similar so it would have been easy for you to mistake the nymph you saw in Viroconium for any of them, especially in the dark. It's a long time since I've seen her, but I don't think she'll have changed much.'

Jack wondered if Myryl would be better tempered than Jennet.

'You know I'm not sure Myryl will be able to help us,' said Elan. 'I've been thinking about it since yesterday. We're a long way from Viroconium.'

'It's the only lead we've got. We'll have to wait and see what she says… if Camelin can find her,' replied Nora.

Just then Camelin circled above them and croaked: 'Let's get started then. I know where she is.'

They put their wellingtons on. Jack and Elan lifted the dustbin out of the car and Nora picked up the wrapped cauldron plate. Camelin flew ahead to show them the way. They had to walk carefully down a track by the side of the field; it was quite muddy after the rain. Camelin landed in a nearby tree and waited for them to catch up.

'I think it would be better if you hid the dustbin behind that big tree over there, it will only distract her if she sees it straight away,' said Nora.

Jack and Elan made sure the dustbin couldn't be seen, and then followed Nora to the edge of the spring. She knelt down and put her lips to the water. Jack could just make out the words through the sound of the bubbles.

'Myryl, you have visitors.'

'That should bring her out!' laughed Elan.

They didn't have long to wait before the water began to gurgle. Steam burst from each bubble as it rose to the surface. A column of water exploded from the pool then subsided. In its place stood a smiling water nymph. As soon as Jack saw Myryl's hair he realised his mistake. It was a lot darker than Jennet's, more of a bottle green, and she didn't seem to have so many stray bits of weed and twigs attached to it either.

She was smaller too and not as slender, but she had the same green skin and strange slanting eyes. The biggest difference was her friendliness.

'Myryl…' Nora began but got no further before she was interrupted.

'Oh how wonderful, visitors, I love visitors!'

Myryl nodded to Nora then made an exaggerated curtsey towards Elan. She seemed genuinely pleased to see them. Nora tried again.

'Do you have…?'

'Well how long has it been?' Myryl said hurriedly. 'It must be a few hundred years since we last spoke, doesn't time fly?'

Nora opened her mouth again to speak but once more Myryl got there first.

'Well this is an unexpected pleasure. The last people who were here started digging up my bog. Stole one of my best cauldrons they did, won't see that again in a hurry. Never even asked, never even attempted to exchange. So rude! The first I knew about it was when I saw them making off with it across the fields. Now let me see, yes, it must have been about a hundred years ago now. Some others came too you know, they were going to build on the mound. Dropped their bells in the lake when they saw me, I frightened them off good and proper. Never came back. Lovely bells they are too, heavy, nice of them to leave them for me don't you think? They're not the same as cauldrons though, didn't really make up for the loss of my best one. Did I tell you about that?'

At last she paused for breath and Nora managed to speak.

'It's cauldrons we've come about, we hear you're the expert and…'

Myryl looked excited and without waiting to hear what Nora was about to ask she told them about all the different kinds of cauldrons she had in her possession. At the next pause Nora managed to complete her question.

'We were wondering if you had anything like this in your collection?' she said hurriedly as she unwrapped the package.

Myryl sniffed the air and thrust her head forward to inspect the cauldron plate more closely.

'That's an old one, not worth anything at all, not if it's not complete. I don't bother with the bits, only the whole ones.'

Myryl reached out and ran her long green fingers over the embossed tree. Elan put her hand on Myryl's to gain her attention,

'Maybe someone gave you three of these a couple of thousand years ago and you've got them somewhere in your collection?'

'They wouldn't have been any use to me. I really don't think I've got any bits but I'll go and have a look.'

Myryl disappeared in a fountain of bubbles into the depths of her watery home.

'Do you think she has them?' asked Jack.

'No,' said Elan. 'I think we need to ask her if she's ever been to Viroconium before we go any further.'

Nora agreed.

'Did you recognise her?' asked Elan.

'It's definitely not her. The one I saw wasn't friendly. I know it was only for a moment but the nymph in the spring at Viroconium was, well, aggressive.'

'And strong,' Camelin added. 'And obviously fond of armour. I wouldn't be surprised if the nymph we're looking for has quite a collection of her own. But I bet it's not cauldrons.'

'You might be right,' replied Nora. 'We'll ask her when she comes back.'

It wasn't long before Myryl resurfaced. She had several pieces of metal in her hand, which she tossed on the grass in front of Nora's feet. They gathered round eagerly to see what she'd brought.

'These are the only bits I've got.'

Most of the metal pieces had been parts of shields. They were rusted and bent. There wasn't anything remotely like the cauldron plate Nora had in her hand. She carefully put them in a pile and Jack handed them back to Myryl who unceremoniously dropped them back into the water.

'I only like complete cauldrons. Doesn't matter what size or shape but I must say I do like the bigger ones, you can't seem to get a good cauldron these days.'

Before Myryl could take another breath, Elan quickly distracted her and asked about the spring at Viroconium.

'Ooooh no!' Myryl shrieked. 'I never went anywhere near that horrible place, those Romans built a whole fortress around the spring in there you know, ruined the view, I stayed as far away from Romans as I could, they frightened all the people off from here you know, I suppose they did me a favour, it's been nice and quiet since they all left but you just don't get the visitors anymore, no one throws anything in the spring, my collection of cauldrons is getting worn out.'

At last Myryl stopped for breath.

Jack thought water nymphs must have incredible lungs to be able to say so much in one sentence.

'Do you know who might have been at Viroconium?' asked Elan before Myryl could tell them about her cauldron collection again.

'Oh yes. That would be Coriss, always was one for swords and daggers.'

It was a surprise when Myryl didn't continue. Her silence had an air of expectancy about it. Nora smiled.

'We have something for you in exchange for your valuable information.'

Jack realised Myryl had been waiting for her gift, but unlike Jennet, she'd been too polite to ask. He went with Elan to collect the dustbin from where they'd hidden it.

'Is this acceptable?' asked Nora. 'We'd hoped you'd have the cauldron plates but your information has been just as valuable.'

Myryl's smile widened, Jack could see a row of bright green teeth.

'This is wonderful, so kind of you. I've never seen anything like it before, it must be very valuable. I don't know anyone else who's got anything like this.'

Nora smiled as Myryl picked up the dustbin and hugged it.

'There is just one last thing before we go; where can we find Coriss?'

Myryl frowned in thought.

'Now, I can't say for sure. In fact, the last time I saw her must have been a few hundred years ago. She's not on speaking terms with many of us, she likes her own company. She was very insulting last time she was here, said I talked too much. I ask you.'

Jack and Camelin had to stop themselves from laughing.

'Who do you think would know where Coriss is now?' asked Elan.

Myryl screwed up her face and started muttering to herself. Jack could hear a few of the names Jennet had read to them from her list. Eventually she nodded thoughtfully before replying.

'Jennet might know, she sends out her Bogie friends to spy on us. She likes to know where everyone is and what they're doing, but it's mainly so she can check up to make sure none of us are more beautiful than she thinks she is. Always was very vain you know, thinks a lot about herself, and so bad tempered all the time.'

Jack was inclined to agree with Myryl; her description of Jennet was very accurate.

'What about Uriel?' asked Nora.

Myryl clutched her dustbin and shook her head vigorously.

'You don't want to go disturbing her, she's dangerous.'

There was a lot of head shaking but Myryl wouldn't say any more.

Nora carefully wrapped the cauldron plate.

'We'd better be going.'

'So soon,' replied Myryl, seeming genuinely disappointed that they were leaving. 'We've hardly had any time to chat, you haven't even told me any of your news.'

'Another time,' replied Nora.

'Anytime you want to visit just stop by. I've always got time to have a chat and it's so nice to have visitors, especially when they bring such wonderful gifts. Don't forget, come again soon.'

Jack was sure she was still speaking as she disappeared with the dustbin in a surge of bubbles.

Nora sat down on the edge of the well.

'I feel quite exhausted after all that!'

Camelin flew down and landed at Nora's feet.

'Now you know how I feel when Timmery comes calling, he talks as much as she does.'

'He's not that bad,' laughed Elan.

'He is when he starts at two o'clock in the morning.'

'What's brought all this on?' asked Nora. 'I thought you two had worked out your differences.'

'So did I, but he came calling again this morning wanting to talk when I was trying to sleep.'

'I expect he only wanted to hear all about your journey into the past again,' said Elan kindly.

'Well I told him I don't have visitors until after breakfast.'

'Why don't you go over to the bell tower at dusk,' suggested Nora. 'You won't be tired then and you can tell Timmery and Charkle all about your adventures again.'

'It's going to be dusk by the time we get back. Can I go with him?' asked Jack.

Nora nodded.

'I'm sure they'll be pleased to see you both. But don't be too long, you've got school in the morning. Elan and I will try to work out a way to speak to Uriel. We must find Coriss soon.'

'Can we fly for a while?' Camelin asked when they were nearly home. 'We can go straight over to see

Timmery and Charkle instead of having to go back to
Ewell House.'

'No detours,' Nora told him.

'No, we'll come straight back from the belfry after
we've seen them.'

'Off you go then,' said Nora once Jack had
transformed.

It was a perfect evening for flying and a relief to be
out in the open after the stuffiness of the car. As Jack
soared upwards he gulped the fresh air. It was lovely to
feel the breeze through his feathers. Nora's car snaked
its way along the country lanes but he lost sight of it as
he followed Camelin across the fields. Jack realised how
lucky he was to be able to fly. Everything that had taken
place since he'd come to live with Grandad had happened
so fast, he'd not really had time to enjoy the sensation of
flying. But tonight was different, it felt good.

'Can we do this again once we've got the plates
back and everything's been sorted out?' he called to
Camelin.

'Course we can, anytime you like. There's nothing
like going for an evening flight, especially at this time
of year.'

The bell tower of the church where Timmery and
Charkle roosted came into sight. He knew Timmery

would be pleased to see them. The little bat, like Myryl, really did enjoy visitors.

As they circled the bell tower, Camelin called to Timmery and Charkle. There was no answer. Once they'd landed Camelin called again.

'Doesn't look like they're in. Now where do you suppose they've gone?' Camelin said.

'I didn't think we'd be coming straight here. I thought you might have something else in mind!'

'Me!'

'Well if they're not here we might as well go back.'

'If they're not here we might have a little chat first.'

Jack looked at Camelin.

'You knew they wouldn't be here didn't you?'

Camelin tried to give Jack his innocent look.

'Timmery told me this morning he was off with Charkle at dusk; he's helping him to look for his family, so I knew we could be alone up here and not be overheard.'

'And?'

'And how about, after you're in your room, I come over and we go for a little night flight? It's a great night for flying, what d'you say? No one will miss you.'

Jack thought for a while. He didn't like going behind Grandad's back but he was also certain Grandad wouldn't miss him.

'Alright, but not for too long, I've got school in the morning.'

'It'll just be a little night flight, a bit of fun, you'll be back in bed before you know it. Come on, the sooner you get home, the sooner we can go out again. But let me do the talking back at Ewell House.'

Nora and Elan were deep in conversation in the library when Jack came down from the loft.

'Back so soon?' said Nora.

'They weren't there, we'll have to try again later,' replied Camelin as he winked at Jack.

'I'll be going now,' Jack called. 'See you tomorrow.'

Nora and Elan left the pile of books and papers and came to say goodbye.

'We really are very grateful, you know, for everything you've done. We'd never have got this far without you,' Nora told him.

'We will get the missing plates back, won't we?'

'We will, it's just a matter of time.'

Elan put her hand on his shoulder.

'Hopefully we'll be luckier tomorrow. I'll meet you in the same place after school.'

Jack turned to Nora.

'What am I going to say to Grandad?'

'Don't worry. I'll go and see him in the morning and tell him we're taking you to visit one of my friends. Which is true in a way, except that I haven't spoken to her for a few hundred years. But we don't have to tell your grandad that bit.'

'Thanks. I'll see you after school.'

Jack waved when he reached the hedge before stepping through the gap and making his way, through the tunnel, to Grandad's garden. It was as airless in the tunnel as it had been in the car. All Jack could think about was the fun he was going to have later, flying in the cool air, with Camelin. There might even be some supper. The Chinese take-away was always open late. After everything he'd been through he thought he deserved a bit of fun.

NIGHT FLIGHT

Jack kept watch from his bedroom window. As the light began to fade, a familiar black shape appeared in the sky.

'He's here,' Jack told Orin. 'I won't be gone long.'

'Ready?' Camelin croaked as he hopped in through Jack's window.

'Ready. If we transform under the blanket we won't light up the whole house.'

Before leaving, Camelin hopped onto the dressing table and had a good look at himself in the mirror. When he was satisfied he turned and inspected Jack.

'You look a lot better without those two feathers sticking up. That singeing really improved your plumage.'

Jack looked in the mirror. Maybe Camelin was right, his feathers were nice and flat now and the bald spot didn't show too much. When he turned around Camelin was already out of the window; seconds later Jack was airborne too.

'Race you to the belfry,' croaked Camelin.

Jack let Camelin fly on ahead. He was enjoying the freedom and the stillness of the night. By the time he landed in the bell tower Timmery and Charkle were already flittering around Camelin's head.

'So kind of you to call, so nice to have visitors; Charkle and I were just going out but we'll stay and have a chat. We've got lots of time.'

Charkle sighed.

'We're still looking for my family.'

'I'm sure you'll find them eventually,' said Jack.

'You might have lots of time but we haven't. Jack's not supposed to be out. I thought I'd take him to the other side of Glasruhen.'

'Oooh! Can we come too? We haven't checked out any of the roosts on the south side.'

'No you can't. This is a raven night out. We only called in to say hello and now we're saying goodbye.'

Both bats looked disappointed and neither of them spoke. Before Jack could say anything, Camelin hopped onto the ledge.

'Come on Jack, time to fly.'

Jack didn't follow Camelin immediately. He didn't like to leave so abruptly.

'If we see anyone in Glasruhen I'll ask them about your family. And we'll come back and have a long chat soon, I promise.'

Jack took off and had to beat his wings powerfully to catch up with Camelin.

'What's on the south side?'

'You'll see.'

'We're not going to be long are we?'

'Naw, just a quick look, I want to check something out. We're doing a bit of investigating. If I'm right it'll save us a lot of time tomorrow night and everyone will be pleased with us. At least, they'll be pleased with me... we can't tell Nora you were here.'

From the air both sides of Glasruhen looked the same to Jack. Camelin circled a few times before he started his descent.

'We'll try down there first, it looks about right.'

'Right for what?'

'To find what we're looking for.'

Before Jack could ask any more, Camelin disappeared into the treetops. Jack followed.

'Over here, but don't make a noise. I don't want anyone to know we're here.'

'Where's here?'

'Uriel's well.'

'Didn't Myryl warn us to stay away from Uriel?'

'We're not going to disturb her, just have a look. When you left, I listened in on Nora and Elan. They had the old map out and Nora said Uriel had to be on the south side somewhere but it might take a while to find her. So I thought if we checked it out tonight, and worked out where she was, it'd save a lot of time.'

'That's a great idea, but how d'you know it's Uriel's well?'

'Remember what Myryl said about her being dangerous? If that's true, there won't be any other water nymph living anywhere near her.'

'It doesn't look like anyone lives here at all.'

'We're looking for a spring with crystal clear water. Nymphs don't live in water that's not fit to drink.'

Jack peered through the trees. They were above a circular pool. There were five grass-covered mounds around one side and a sheer rock face on the other. The place looked eerie in the moonlight. There wasn't a ripple on the surface of the water.

'Is this it?'

'Naw, this is the pool the spring runs into, we need to be a bit higher. But it's pure water, look at all the reeds and moss. Come on, but keep quiet.'

Jack followed Camelin through the trees. They landed on the ground in front of an old well, which had been carved out of the rock. The only sound was the trickle of water over the mossy rocks. This was the first well Jack had seen that didn't have any trees growing nearby. The feathers on the back of his neck stood on end, he felt a shiver run down his spine. He'd felt like this before, the day he thought he was being watched on the back lane. Only this time it was dark and he was a long way from Grandad's.

'Let's go,' he whispered.

'Not yet, I need to make sure this is Uriel's well.'

There was a slight movement. Jack peered into the gloom. He was sure he could see a pair of eyes. Camelin didn't seem to have noticed, he was too busy poking the moss around the base of the well with his beak.

'It's a bit overgrown but someone definitely still lives here so it's got to be Uriel.'

As soon as Camelin said Uriel's name again the rock quivered. There was a hissing sound and the eyes Jack thought he'd seen blinked.

'Who wantsss to know?'

Jack gasped. The moonlight lit the side of the rock and revealed a grotesque face, its wide gaping mouth snapped shut, and a forked tongue flicked out. The stone creature fixed Jack with its cold cruel eyes.

'I asssked you, who wantsss to know?'

Jack could feel his legs trembling. He wanted to fly but he couldn't move. His body felt rigid, he was too frightened to speak.

'Don't look at her!' Camelin shouted as he shielded his eyes with his wing.

'What… is… it?' Jack stuttered. 'What's happening?'

He tried to shield his own eyes, but his wing wouldn't move. He was transfixed.

'Come on Jack, time to go.'

'I can't move. It won't take its eyes off me.'

'Release him.'

'Why should I? No one asssked you to come and disssturb usss. Grol wake up, we've got visssitorsss.'

Another creature on the other side of the well stirred.

'Did I hear you right Agye, visssitorsss? What you caught there?'

'A raven; we've not had bird for agesss, much better than micesss.'

Jack swallowed hard. He should never have let Camelin persuade him to go for a night flight. If he couldn't move, how was he going to get back to Grandad's? Would he ever get back if these creatures intended to eat him?

'Can't you do something Camelin?'

'We've come to see Uriel,' Camelin announced.

There was silence. Jack wasn't sure this was the best idea. If Uriel appeared they might be in more danger than they were already.

'No one speaksss to Uriel unlesss we say so,' hissed Grol.

'We need to see your gift first,' added Agye.

'We haven't got a gift.'

'Then you lie,' she screeched. 'Nobody disturbsss a water nymph without a gift.'

'I say they were spying, what do you say Agye?'

'Spying it isss. Them that tell liesss we getsss to keep and eat, they don't come bothering usss no more then.'

'Release him,' piped a small voice from above the well.

'Timmery!' exclaimed Jack.

'And Charkle,' said another shrill voice.

'Don't look in her eyes, either of you,' shouted Camelin. 'Go get Nora, she'll sort them out.'

'We don't need to, everything's under control,' said Charkle.

Jack didn't feel things were under control. He didn't want Nora to know he'd sneaked out, they'd both be in trouble if she found out, but the kind of trouble they'd be in with Nora would be better than the kind they were in now.

'Release him,' Timmery shouted in his loudest voice. 'Or else!'

Grol and Agye sounded like a steam engine as they both exploded in laughter.

'Don't you know who we are?' asked Grol.

'You're gargoyles,' replied Timmery. 'Seen plenty of your kind but never had the pleasure of speaking to one before.'

'At last someone who knowsss usss,' laughed Agye. 'So you'll know we ain't frightened of a couple of small batsss and a fat raven. There's nothing you could do to harm usss.'

Jack could hear whispering behind his back.

'Brilliant!' exclaimed Camelin. 'Don't worry Jack. We'll have you free in no time.'

Grol and Agye rocked from side to side as they laughed even harder. Jack heard a fluttering of wings.

'I need your help Jack,' shouted Camelin. 'I'm

coming in with my eyes closed so you'll have to guide me. Let me know if I'm on target.'

Jack had no idea what was about to happen. Grol and Agye struggled for breath in between their fits of laughter. They laughed even more when a blob of mud splattered Agye on the nose.

'Ooooh! That hurt!' she chortled.

'You're going to have to think of something better than that!' shouted Grol.

'Where did it land?' asked Camelin.

'Bang on her nose.'

Camelin flew over again and Jack watched as he shot a beak-full of mud at Agye again.

'Smack in her eyes,' Jack shouted excitedly when he realised Camelin was trying to block out her gaze. He tried to move but he could still feel Agye's intense stare through the mud. Grol continued laughing as mud slid down Agye's face.

'Fire three!' commanded Timmery.

'Right on target,' Jack called. 'But it keeps sliding…'

Before he could finish, a flame engulfed Agye's stony face. Jack could hear a high-pitched wail. Grol's mouth fell open, he wasn't laughing any more. Jack felt his body go limp as he collapsed to the ground.

'Are you OK?' Camelin asked.

'I think so.'

'What you done to her?' Grol hissed. 'Releassse her.'

'Not bad for two little bats and a fat raven!' laughed Camelin.

'Do something Grol, this mud's rock hard. I can't see a thing.'

'Like what?'

Camelin paced up and down in front of the well.

'We could make a bargain and I'll come and peck two eye holes for you. But if you break your word we'll be back.'

'Anything, anything you say.' Agye hissed.

'First, you must promise never to freeze ravens again.'

'Or bats and rats,' added Timmery.

'I promisesss.'

'Second, we need some information, which is why we needed to speak to Uriel in the first place.'

'She won't see you, she doesn't see anyone. We deal with visssitorsss.'

'Well let's hope you can help. We need to know where to find Coriss.'

'Not seen her for yearsss,' said Grol. 'But I know who would know. You need to go and find yourself a

66

Bogie, they're the only onesss who know that kind of stuff.'

'We've already seen a Bogie, that's why we came to see Uriel. Someone must know where Coriss lives.'

'What about a Dorysk? You'd have to catch one firssst, and they won't give you information unless you've got something to trade.'

'A Dorysk!' exclaimed Camelin. 'Now why didn't I think of that before?'

'Is he telling the truth?' asked Jack.

'He isss, he isss,' screeched Agye. 'Now give me back my eyesss.'

'I'll peck the holes,' Jack told Camelin. 'If they try to double cross us you can sort her out again, you've got a better aim than me.'

'Won't double crossss, we promissse.'

Jack hopped back in front of the well when he'd finished pecking two holes into the hardened mud. It looked as if Agye was wearing a mask but at least she didn't transfix him again.

'Come on,' said Camelin. 'Let's go and find ourselves a Dorysk.'

'What's a Dorysk?' asked Jack.

Camelin tutted loudly, 'Don't you know anything?'

They took off in the direction of Newton Gill. As they left, Grol and Agye were still grumbling. After a while, the only sound in the night was the flapping and fluttering of wings.

'Thank you,' Jack said after his legs had stopped trembling. 'It was lucky you two came along when you did.'

Camelin humphed and gave the bats a glower.

'I don't think luck has much to do with it. We were followed, weren't we?'

'You said we could go on an adventure with you, and we wanted to find out what you were up to,' Timmery replied.

'We thought we could look for Norris and Snook at the same time,' continued Charkle. 'Maybe we could ask the Dorysk if it knows where any Dragonettes have been seen lately. That's if you catch one.'

'What d'you mean, if I catch one! I'll have you know I can spot a Dorysk no matter how hard it tries to disguise itself, but they'll only answer one question. You'll have to catch your own if you want to ask about your family. And make sure you have something to trade or you'll not get an answer at all.'

'Would someone please tell me what a Dorysk is?'

They all looked at Jack. Camelin sighed.

'Dorysks are a bit like Bogies, they spy and trade information. Unlike Bogies they can shape shift, but only into something about the same size or smaller, nothing bigger.'

'Do they like shiny things like water nymphs?'

'They'll trade for anything that takes their fancy but they mainly they like sharp things, like pins. Some of them are pin millionaires.'

Jack had no idea why anyone would want a million pins. He wondered how big a Dorysk was and hoped it was going to be friendly.

'What's Nora going to say when she finds out where we've been and what happened?'

Camelin looked at them all in turn.

'Nora isn't going to find out, is she? No one breathes a word. Promise?'

'Promise,' they agreed.

'It'll be our secret,' piped Timmery.

'Yes, a secret,' agreed Camelin.

'So what does a Dorysk look like?' continued Jack.

'Depends what shape it's in. Don't know why I didn't think of a Dorysk, I should have gone hunting for one before. We'd have had the cauldron remade by now. The problem is, they're not very easy to catch.'

Jack didn't ask any more questions. He was worried about getting back to Grandad's, it must be late by now and he'd got to get up in the morning for school. He didn't like to ask how long it would take to find a Dorysk.

They were at the edge of Newton Gill Forest when Camelin started to descend. He made his way towards what used to be an ash tree. Its leafless branches were rotten and creaked as they landed.

'What do we do now?' asked Jack.

'Act suspicious, do something unusual. That will always bring a Dorysk out. They're even nosier than Bogies.'

'Couldn't we go back now? Nora's going to find out you know, the trees will tell her.'

'Not these. Don't you remember, dead wood don't talk? The only thing the trees and Nora are talking about at the moment is Arrana. She hasn't got time for tittle-tattle, she's too busy worrying.'

Jack was worried too. He knew time was running out. They all sat on the branch, no one moved and no one did anything unusual. Jack wondered if they were going to be there all night, and then Camelin started his shuffle dance. Jack decided to join in. Unfortunately, the branch wasn't strong enough to support a lot of bouncing up and down. There was a loud crack that echoed round the forest; then the branch came down. No one was hurt but it sent all the creatures on the ground scurrying away, except for one.

'Got you!' cried Camelin as he grabbed a large beetle in his claw.

'Let me go you big bully,' a small voice replied.

'I'm not a bully. I'm just good at catching Dorysks.'

'Alright, you recognised me. You get to ask your question.'

Camelin released the beetle. In a flash it shape shifted into what looked like a large hedgehog. It had prickles all over its body except for its face. On the end of its nose was a small pair of glasses. It shuffled and snuffled around Jack's feet, until eventually, it sat on its haunches and sighed before speaking.

'Let's get down to business then.'

'Business!' exclaimed Jack.

'Don't worry,' said Camelin as he stepped in front of Jack. 'I'm in charge here.'

There was a tittering from Timmery and Charkle, which Camelin chose to ignore.

'What have you got to trade?'

'We didn't come to trade, we're visiting. Jack's new to the area and I'm showing him around.'

'So why'd you catch me?'

'I wanted Jack to meet the most knowledgeable Dorysk in the West.'

'Only the West? I think you'll find I'm the most well informed Dorysk in the whole kingdom.'

'I told you he was famous,' Camelin said as he turned to Jack.

'If you're visiting, where've you been?'

'Uriel's well.'

The bats and Jack nodded. The Dorysk looked shocked.

'Uriel's well! No one goes there!'

'Jack hadn't seen gargoyles before, I told you he's visiting. We're off to see Coriss next.'

'At the Mere Pool?'

'Yes, at the Mere Pool. Now we really must be

going, we've got a lot of other places to go to before daybreak.'

The Dorysk looked thoughtful. It ran its sharp claws through the dead leaves, found a maggot, flipped it in the air and gulped it down.

'Care for one?' he asked Jack.

'No thank you. We ate before we came out and we really need to be going now.'

'No matter,' the Dorysk replied as he dug out another maggot. 'I'm sure we'll meet again another time.'

'You were brilliant,' Jack told Camelin once they were airborne.

'They're not very clever, you know, not as clever as ravens.'

'Do you think he realised you'd tricked him?'

'Naw, he'll be tucking into those maggots now and won't give us another thought. Come on, we'd better get you back to your room.'

Timmery and Charkle said goodnight when they reached Grandad's house.

'Let us know when you're off out again, we'd like to come with you,' piped Timmery.

'Maybe you could come and help us search for my brothers,' added Charkle.

'Once the cauldron is remade and everything's been sorted out we'll come and help you, won't we Camelin?' said Jack.

Camelin grumbled to himself.

'We will,' Jack assured Charkle. 'I've got to go now or I'll never get up in the morning.'

'See you after school then,' said Camelin once Jack had transformed and was in his pyjamas.

Jack yawned, but before he could answer, Camelin was gone. Once Jack was in bed Orin came and lay down next to him on the pillow. She said something, but Jack was too sleepy to go and find his wand.

'It's been quite a night,' he told her. 'I don't think I'll be going on any more night flights but at least we know where Coriss is now. I'll tell you all about it in the morning.'

Jack closed his eyes. He couldn't keep them open any longer.

THE MERE POOL

Jack could hear Grandad calling him from downstairs. He forced his eyes open but they promptly closed again. Orin nudged his ear with her nose, but even though he knew she was hungry, and wanted her breakfast, he couldn't get out of bed.

The knock on his bedroom door meant he must have fallen asleep again.

'Jack, are you up? If you don't get a move on you'll be late.'

'Won't be long,' Jack replied as he swung his feet out of bed.

The next half hour was frantic as Jack washed, dressed, fed Orin and bolted his breakfast. By the time he got to school he felt exhausted. He didn't remember much about any of the morning lessons, he'd dozed through most of them. Luckily, nobody seemed to notice.

At lunchtime, Jack got permission to use the library. He found a quiet corner and got out his Book of Shadows. He hoped there'd be a message waiting for him and wasn't disappointed. He waited eagerly for the words to appear:

dont tell Nora or Elan you no abowt the

dont for get it's a see kret

Jack laughed when he'd read Camelin's message.

He wondered if he could magic a spell checker into Camelin's book for him. He was about to write back when another message appeared:

We know where Coriss is.
Camelin caught a Dorysk last night and found out for us.
Nora and I have thought of a special gift for her,
one she won't be able to resist.

Jack looked around to see if anyone was watching before he took his wand and answered both messages. To Camelin he wrote:

I won't forget.

And to Elan:

What's a Dorysk?

He wondered if he might learn any more from her, but she told him to look in his Book of Shadows and said Camelin would tell him all about it on the way to the Mere Pool later.

The afternoon went quickly. Jack felt fine by the time he met Elan, and they were soon on their way to see Coriss. Jack looked over the seat into the back of the car. The picnic basket was there, along with the wrapped cauldron plate and another package about the same shape and size as the base plate of the cauldron.

'Has Camelin flown on ahead?'

'In here,' came a muffled reply from the picnic basket.

'He's been very quiet in there,' said Nora. 'I think he's crumb hunting!'

'So where are we going?'

'Camelin will tell you all about his meeting with the Dorysk. He was really lucky to find one, they're masters of disguise and very hard to catch,' explained Elan.

'It wasn't easy. I was out for hours scouring the countryside.'

'You'll never believe what happened. He tricked the Dorysk into telling him where to find Coriss,' added Elan.

'I'm telling Jack, not you. Can I come out now?'

Camelin lifted one of the flaps and poked his head out. Jack held it open so he could hop out.

'Are we going far?'

'Naw, it's just the other side of Beconbury. We'll be there in no time.'

Camelin was right. It wasn't long before Nora turned off the main road into a small country lane and then into a car park. Instead of parking near the other cars, Nora drove towards the opposite end before switching the engine off. They were next to a low stile. A damaged signpost indicated the way to the Mere Pool. Not far away, Jack could see small boats bobbing around on a lake. Several sailing dinghies with brightly coloured sails sped through the water.

'Ready?' asked Nora as she picked up the cauldron plate and passed the other package to Jack.

'Ready,' they replied.

'I presume we're going somewhere a bit quieter,' said Jack.

'We are,' agreed Nora. 'Camelin will show us the way.'

The Mere Pool was secluded and overgrown. It was surrounded by tall slender trees whose leaves quivered in the gentle breeze. The water in the pool was still, apart from an occasional ripple moving across the surface. It looked deep and forbidding, Jack was glad he wasn't alone.

Nora stopped by the water's edge. Instead of kneeling down and putting her lips to the water she took a heavy coin from her pocket and flipped it into the pool.

'That should bring her up,' she laughed. 'I doubt anyone's thrown a Roman coin in there for a while.'

Nothing happened. Jack began to wonder if the Dorysk had played his own trick on them and given them the wrong information. Maybe the coin Nora had thrown in wasn't acceptable, it was quite dull.

'I thought nymphs liked shiny things?'

'They do but we need to tempt her out. She'll want to know who's throwing dirty coins in her pool. She'll be up soon,' explained Nora.

'She's got a worse temper than Jennet,' added Elan. 'If she thinks we're desperate for something she won't let us have it. It's really going to depend on how much she likes the gift we've brought. I'm hoping she'll think it's so special that she'll let us have the cauldron plates without too much bother.'

Jack was worried. If this was the same nymph he'd seen in the spring at Viroconium she wasn't going to want to chat like Myryl. He hoped she liked the gift. After all, he was the one who had to offer it to her.

'What if she doesn't like it or she's got one already? She must have thousands of shiny things down there after all these years.'

'She will have,' agreed Nora. 'But I'm sure what we've brought will be the best gift she's ever had.'

Jack got a shock when Coriss finally decided to surface. He'd only seen nymphs rising from small springs or wells before. This time was different. Surrounded by a mass of bubbles, Coriss used the whole pool. The water began to swirl and spiral downwards, and a black hole appeared in the centre, out of which, a sword began to rise. The last time Jack had seen that sword, the Camp Prefect of Viroconium had been holding it in his hand. Now, pale green fingers gripped the hilt tightly. A faded red plume came into view – a little the worse for wear and with quite a lot of weed attached to it.

'It's her!' Jack gasped.

He was amazed to see she was wearing the fish scaled armour he'd also seen on the Prefect. It looked strange to see her pale green skin underneath it instead of a red tunic. There was no doubt in his mind.

They'd found the nymph he'd mistaken for Jennet at Viroconium.

'AVE!' Coriss shouted as she made a fist with her free hand and beat it on her armour. 'Who comes here disturbing my peace?'

She pulled something out of the plume of her helmet and flipped it towards Nora.

'I don't take kindly to people throwing worthless things into my pool. If you've come for something, speak out, and it had better be worth my while.'

The coin rolled to a stop at Nora's feet. Instead of picking it up Nora smiled before slightly bowing her head.

'What marvellous armour and such amazing weaponry. Very impressive!'

Coriss straightened and thrust her shoulders back before bowing back.

'It's a matching set. The most magnificent gift I've ever had. Never had another gift like it, don't expect I ever will.'

'Is it Roman?' asked Nora.

'And why would you want to know that?'

'We've been searching the land for the nymph who once lived in the spring at Viroconium. Many years ago she was given some armour as a gift.'

'And why would anyone be wanting such a nymph?'

'We have sworn to search until we find her. We have something belonging to that nymph, and she has something which belongs to us. We would like to undertake an exchange.'

Coriss looked thoughtful. Nora stood to one side so Jack could step forward.

'Do you remember this boy?'

Coriss sniffed the air and looked intently at Jack.

Nora patted him encouragingly on the back.

'I gave you three cauldron plates the night you acquired your armour, could I have them back please?'

'In exchange for what? I don't give things back unless I'm offered something much better in return. And even then it depends. I might not want to exchange.'

Nora signalled to Jack to unwrap the circular package.

Coriss thrust her head forward, sniffed the air, then reached for the gift, but Nora took it from Jack and held it high so the sunlight glinted on its surface. Jack could see it was a hubcap from a car. In the centre were the letters VW.

'A shield,' shrieked Coriss. 'Oh how magnificent! But what do the letters mean?'

'They have a very important meaning. They stand for *Viroconium Warrior*. Only the most noble and distinguished may bear this shield.'

'I'll be back,' said Coriss as she promptly disappeared beneath the water.

'That's amazing,' said Jack. 'How did you know she'd want the shield?'

'We didn't,' Elan replied. 'But even if she'd got one we knew it wouldn't have *VW* on it.'

'Do you think she has the plates?'

'Oh yes,' replied Nora. 'She understood exactly what you'd asked her for. She'll turn out every cupboard she has until she finds them.'

They didn't have to wait long for Coriss to reappear. This time there wasn't any whirlpool, or grand entrance, she came straight to the edge of the pool and spoke to Jack.

'Is this what you seek?'

Jack's heart skipped a beat. In her hand were the missing plates. He was too frightened to speak so he nodded vigorously. As she handed them to Jack, Nora gave her the shield. She slipped her hand through a strap, which had been fastened to the back, drew her sword and swaggered to the middle of the pool.

'VIROCONIUM WARRIOR!' she cried before a great surge of bubbles engulfed her. The whole pool began to swirl once more as Coriss slowly disappeared into the black hole in the centre. The last thing they saw was the tip of her sword.

'Show off,' grumbled Camelin.

'It doesn't matter. We got what we came for,' said Nora. 'Now we can remake the cauldron.'

'As soon as we get back?' asked Jack as he and Elan wrapped the cloth around the wet plates.

'Yes,' agreed Nora. 'As soon as we get back.'

'What about supper?' asked Camelin.

'Not until the cauldron's remade, then we'll celebrate,' Nora told him.

'I can't wait to see what it looks like,' replied Jack.

Camelin had already flown off towards home. Jack presumed he'd be taking in a food stop on the way; he obviously didn't want to have to wait for his supper.

'She really liked the shield,' he said as they walked back across the field.

'She must be really proud of her armour. Did you notice how well she'd looked after it,' replied Elan.

'It looks better on her than it did on the Camp Prefect,' chuckled Jack.

'We've got something important to discuss before you go home tonight but Camelin will need to be there too,' said Nora.

Jack felt excited; it wouldn't be long before they could go into Annwn.

When they arrived back at Ewell House, Camelin was waiting for them on the picnic table. Jack was sure he could see some cheese stuck to his beak. Nora went straight into the herborium. Jack followed her and watched as she put the last three plates into position. She ran her hands over each one of them in turn.

'At last! This is wonderful, after all the years of waiting. And it's all down to you Jack.'

'And Camelin, I couldn't have done it without his help.'

'And Camelin,' agreed Nora. 'Would you go and fetch him, then we can make a start?'

As he left the herborium Jack searched his pockets for a tissue.

'Nora wants you, but you can't go in with a blob of cheese on your beak. Hold still while I wipe it off.'

'Pizza cheese is so sticky, it gets everywhere. I've been trying to get it off.'

Jack cleaned Camelin's beak.

'Thanks, I'd have been in trouble if Nora had seen it.'

'Come on. Nora's waiting to lace the plates together.'

'I can't wait to go into Annwn. You can eat as much as you want there and it's all free, you don't have to pay for anything. Gwillam used to tell me about the pies, he said they melted in your mouth. And the sausages were the best he'd ever tasted. They have a fair at festival time and a big market with lots of stalls. Gwillam said there are story tellers, jugglers, games, races and singing at night round the home fires. There will be so much to see and do when we get there. I hope we can stay for a while.'

'It sounds great.'

'Oh it is. The Citadel's on an island. I want to go across the river to see the Glass Palace. Gwillam told me there are white ravens in the Queen's garden. What do you think Jack? Was he joking or do you think there really are white ravens?'

'I don't see why not. It all sounds amazing, I can't wait to see it for myself.'

'Come on you two,' Elan called from the herborium. 'We're ready to begin.'

'I'm afraid we need to ask you to help again Jack,' Nora began. 'My powers are fading fast. I don't want to waste them on things I know you can do.'

'But I don't have the same kind of power as you.'

'When you know all there is to know you will, I assure you. But for now I need you to find the pages we need from my Book of Shadows.'

'What about me?' asked Camelin. 'Will I have a lot of power too?'

'You are a Druid's acolyte. When you've finished your training you'll have magic too.'

'But that'll take years,' grumbled Camelin.

'What do you want me to do?' asked Jack.

'We need the instructions for binding the cauldron. I probably remember them correctly, but it's been so long since I've done it, I'd rather make sure we get it right. Here's your wand, I need you to help me remake it.'

Elan got Nora's Book of Shadows from the bookshelf and put it in front of Jack. His wand immediately turned smooth once it was in his right hand. He concentrated hard and let all his thoughts travel to the tip of his wand before tapping the book.

It opened with a bang as the covers hit the table.

'You're a natural Jack,' said Elan as she picked up the book and read the instructions for Nora:

To Bind the Cauldron of Life
Lay the plates around the yew,
First the pine then holly too,
Next the willow and hawthorn take,
Birch, ash, elm, oak are the first eight.
Beech and apple follow then,
Now the plates will number ten.
Hazel and rowan last not least,
Now lace the Cauldron for the feast.

When Nora had finished lacing the plates together she stood back to admire her work. The cauldron was bigger than Jack had expected.

'Now for the rim and handles.'

Elan brought out a solid ring of metal, which had two loops hanging opposite each other. Nora placed it on top of the cauldron then turned to Jack.

'We need the instructions for opening the portal into Annwn.'

'What do I ask?'

'The Western Portal lies hidden in the forest. Say its name and the book will open.'

'But what name should I say?'

'Glasruhen Gate,' replied Elan.

Jack didn't know what the gate looked like but he knew the forest. He concentrated hard and put his wand on the book.

'Glasruhen Gate,' he commanded.

The pages flipped until the book found what Jack had asked for. At the top of the page in ancient writing were the words:

Glasruhen Gate
The Western Portal of Annwn

'What else does it say?' asked Camelin.

Jack handed the book to Elan:

The sacred wells you must locate,
From each collect a cauldron plate.
When they're found and brought together,
Bind them up with thongs of leather.

'We've done that now,' said Camelin. 'Even though it took a long time.'

'What's next?' asked Nora.

Elan continued reading:

> *Tap three times on the cauldron's rim,*
> *Then ready you'll be to begin.*
> *With oak, beech, willow, birch and pine,*
> *And acorn from the Sacred Shrine,*
> *At sunset on the ritual date,*
> *Lay them before Glasruhen Gate.*

'Are you ready Jack?' asked Nora, 'you need to tap the rim three times.'

As Jack tapped, a green light began to radiate from inside. It spread through the plates until the whole cauldron glowed. The leather thongs seemed to melt into the metal and the rim shone brightly until the plates fused together. Jack stood with his mouth open, his heart pounding in his chest.

'You did it. You've remade the cauldron Jack,' Camelin croaked as he hopped around the table. 'We'll be in Annwn in no time now.'

Jack looked at Nora and Elan but neither spoke.

'You can open the portal can't you?'

'We can, with your help,' replied Nora.

'I'll do whatever you want,' said Jack.

'We owe both of you a great deal and there are many who will be grateful to you forever,' added Elan as she exchanged glances with Nora. 'There's something important we have to discuss.'

The tone of her voice told Jack that something was wrong.

'We've had to change our plans, we can't wait until Samhain.'

Camelin hopped around excitedly.

'So when are we going?'

'We're opening the portal tonight. It couldn't be more perfect, they'll be celebrating Midsummer in Annwn.'

'A festival!' cried Camelin. 'How long can we stay?'

Nora sighed.

'I'm sorry, but you won't be able to go.'

'What d'you mean, I won't be able to go? You promised. It's not fair if Jack gets to go and I don't. Not after all we've been through together.'

'Jack can't go either.'

There was silence. Jack wanted to ask why. He too wanted to say that it wasn't fair, but he could see the pain in Nora's eyes. Elan reached over and gently stroked Camelin's feathers.

'We're sorry, but if we don't go soon it will be too late.'

'But why can't we come with you?' asked Camelin.

'Only the Fair Folk or Druids may enter Annwn without permission. Mortals are only allowed to pass through the gate at Samhain, it's the law and we have to obey it.'

'It's a stupid law,' grumbled Camelin.

Jack couldn't speak.

'If you turn over that last page in my book Jack, it might help to explain.'

Jack raised his wand and turned the page. He couldn't see to read for the tears which had welled up in his eyes. Elan took the book from him:

Between the archway will be seen,
A gleaming gateway, tall and green,
No humankind may enter here,
Except at Samhain every year.

The Law of Annwn does decree,
For trespass there's a penalty.
For crimes committed in the Land,
Before the Council you must stand.

'We can't wait until Samhain. We've got to collect the acorns tonight. Arrana is fading fast and my magic is almost gone, I need to drink the elixir. Elan must renew her strength too before it's too late. You do understand don't you, we'd take you with us if we could.'

Jack nodded. Nora and Elan turned to Camelin. He hung his head, and then slowly nodded too.

GLASRUHEN GATE

'It's lucky we didn't have too much trouble getting the plates back this afternoon, we've got a lot to do before sunset,' said Nora. 'We're going to need you both to help.'

Camelin's head slumped. He shuffled down to the end of the table and turned his back on them all. Nora sighed and continued speaking to Jack.

'I know it's a lot to ask, but we're not going to be able to open Glasruhen Gate without you. I need to have some magic in reserve to make the elixir once we're in Annwn.'

'Will you open the gate for us?' asked Elan.

'Me! How can I open the gate?'

'You have all the power in your wand. It began life as an acorn from the Mother Oak in Annwn, the portal will recognise its power and will open to it.'

'So why won't your wands do the same, they came from Annwn didn't they?'

'Ours are earthly wands. Mine's from the hazel tree and Elan's is birch wood,' explained Nora.

Camelin slowly turned.

'You mean my wand's better than yours?'

Nora laughed.

'Yes Camelin, yours and Jack's are both better than ours. Now we've got lots to do. First, Jack will need to go home and ask his grandad if he can stay till later Tell him we're back from visiting and we're going to have a barbecue.'

'A barbecue, a real barbecue?' croaked Camelin as he skipped over to Nora.

'A real barbecue, but not for everyone, just for us. We'll celebrate properly when we get back with the acorns. We're not eating until everything is ready, so you can come and help me cut some rhubarb. Elan can go with Jack.'

'Oh great, I love rhubarb pie.'

'It's not for us, I haven't got time to make pies tonight. It's to take into Annwn. We have to take a gift of something they don't have. They only grow apples, any other kind of fruit is most welcome. The cauldron is the only way of transporting things from this world into Annwn. It will have been a long time since they've had any rhubarb.'

Jack smiled when he saw Camelin begin to sulk again. They parted ways at the dovecot; Nora and Camelin went off to the kitchen garden, while Jack and Elan went down to the hedge.

'I'm really sorry you aren't coming with us,' said Elan as they walked through the yew tree tunnel from Ewell House to Grandad's.

'You will come back, won't you?'

'I will, but there are things I have to do in Annwn. I might not come back with Nora tonight, it depends what we find. I might have to stay a little while.'

'I'm not going to see you as you really are now, am I?'

'You will at Samhain. Once we've opened the portal I'll be free to come and go between Earth and

Annwn. Both you and Camelin can visit in October. It'll be a great birthday present for you.'

'Is it really as wonderful as Camelin says?'

'Even Camelin will be amazed when he sees it. The Citadel and the Palace stand in the middle of a lake, each of its four towers are made of glass and you can see them glinting in the sunlight for miles.'

'Is it true about the white ravens?'

'Yes, it's true. They live in the Queen's garden at the Citadel.'

Jack sighed. The four months before he could go and see everything for himself would pass very slowly. As they emerged from the hedge Grandad looked up from where he was planting peas.

'You're back early. I wasn't expecting you 'til supper time. And you've brought Elan with you.'

'Hello Mr Brenin. I've come to ask if Jack can stay a bit later tonight, we're going to have a barbecue. He'll be home about 10 o'clock, if that's alright?'

'Of course he can, but you'll need to change out of your school clothes, Jack. You don't want them smelling of smoke for school tomorrow, do you?'

Jack left Elan with his grandad in the garden and went upstairs to change. No matter how hard he tried he couldn't help feeling disappointed.

Jack saw Camelin waiting by the rockery when they came back through the hedge.

'You took your time,' he croaked.

'Is there anything we need to do?' asked Elan.

'Naw, we've done it all. Nora said we could start the barbecue as soon as you got back so come on, what you waiting for? It's grub time.'

Camelin took off and flew towards the house. As Jack passed the herborium he noticed a huge bundle of rhubarb, which had been neatly cut into sticks of about the same length, sticking out of the cauldron. By the time they reached the patio Camelin was arguing with Nora.

'But I want to,' he croaked.

'It's too dangerous, you've not had any practice. Let Jack do it.'

Camelin turned to Jack.

'She won't let me light the barbecue. I can do it, I know I can. I've watched you make sparks and I've already made some. Please Jack, please let me try.'

Nora shook her head and looked at Jack. He raised

his hand to the tiny bald spot, where his hair used to stick up.

'It's OK with me if Camelin wants to do it, as long as he points his wand towards the barbecue.'

'Aw Jack, you're a real friend,' said Camelin as he hopped around Jack's legs before diving into the kitchen. Seconds later he was back with his wand.

'Stand back,' warned Nora.

Camelin flew onto the picnic table and then shuffled into position. Jack smiled when he heard Camelin's muffled command.

'Fire one!'

Nora gasped as a great flame shot from the end of Camelin's wand.

'Make it smaller!' she shouted.

'Why? I thought you wanted the fire lit?'

'We do, but not like that! I think I'm going to take charge of your wand while we're gone, it'll be safer.'

Camelin was about to start sulking again but then he caught sight of the tray of sausages in Elan's hand.

'Sausages, my favourite!'

'What happens at the Midsummer Festival in Annwn?' asked Jack.

'It's like any other fair,' replied Elan. 'There'll be a big market with lots of stalls and fun things to do.

All the best storytellers gather there and try to out-do each other. I remember last time there were jugglers, stilt walkers, all kinds of things.'

'See, I told you,' said Camelin as he landed on Jack's shoulder. 'Tell us about the food.'

Nora laughed.

'Is that all you ever think about? Well your supper's ready when you are. You certainly got the charcoal good and hot. This lot's cooked in no time.'

Just before the sun began to sink, Nora made one final check to make sure they'd got everything they needed.

'It's time,' she announced. 'We need to go.'

They set off for Glasruhen Forest. Jack and Elan carried the cauldron between them. His wand and Camelin's were inside it next to the rhubarb stalks. As they passed the hedge Nora picked up a large bundle of branches.

'Oak, beech, willow, birch and pine, for the ritual,' she explained.

'Where exactly is Glasruhen Gate?' asked Jack.

'That I don't know,' replied Nora.

'But how will we find it?'

'My Book of Shadows will guide us to the right place. It'll be somewhere in Glasruhen Forest. It didn't always move about, but when the troubles came the Blessed Council decided, for the safety of Annwn, that the gateways mustn't remain fixed. Only the Sentinel Oaks know the position of the portals.'

'Sentinel Oaks?' asked Jack.

'They guard the four gateways into Annwn, one on either side. It's their branches which form the archway we'll need to pass through.'

Jack didn't really understand what Nora was talking about. When they had left the yew tunnel behind and were approaching the edge of the forest, Nora stopped.

'Here we are, time to swap over. You take my Book of Shadows and I'll carry the cauldron with Elan.'

Jack took Nora's book and she passed him his wand. The two trees on the cover shimmered. They looked alive, more alive than some of the trees in Newton Gill Forest.

'Use it like a compass,' Nora told him. 'Follow the pull, it'll feel like a magnet.'

The book felt as if it had a life of its own and Jack let it lead the way. They went deeper and deeper into the forest. He could feel a hundred eyes watching. Occasionally he caught a glimpse of a Dryad but no one blocked his way or spoke to him.

The book stopped pulling and Jack looked up. He was in front of two ancient oaks. Their branches touched each other, making a natural archway.

'I think we must be here,' he said.

'Well done Jack! I knew you could do it. Now, let's get started, the light is fading fast.'

'But the book said there'd be a tall gleaming gateway. There's nothing like that here.'

'These are the Sentinel Oaks,' said Elan as she laid her hand on the nearest tree trunk. Once upon a time they would have greeted us, but they've been asleep for so long now it would take an age to wake them.'

'Does that mean we can't do the ritual?'

'It's not a problem, don't worry Jack,' Nora assured him. 'With your magic we can open the gateway. Once we've performed the ritual all will be revealed.'

It was alright Nora saying *don't worry*, she'd performed lots of rituals. This was Jack's first and he didn't want anything to go wrong, especially since so much depended on him getting it right.

Elan put her hand on his shoulder.

'If it doesn't work the first time we can try again.

It's not like the window in time. Now you've found it we can keep trying until it opens.'

'Now if you don't mind Jack, can you ask my Book of Shadows for the instructions to get this gateway open?'

Jack's wand felt familiar in his hand now. He pointed it at Nora's book and commanded: 'Show me the instructions for opening Glasruhen Gate.'

The pages turned. Eventually they lay still and Jack read:

Instructions for opening a Portal into Annwn
To open up a Portal wide,
Into Annwn's fair countryside,
The sacred Treasure must be sought,
Then before the Sentinels brought.

'We've done all that,' complained Camelin. 'What's next?'

'It's alright Jack, don't take any notice of him. What else does it say?'

First put five branches in a row,
And say the ritual words you know.
Hold the Treasure from the shrine,
Then let the golden acorn shine.

Jack felt worried.

'I don't know any ritual words…'

'I do,' interrupted Nora. 'All you have to do is will the gateway to appear, I'll say the right words. Just keep concentrating and pointing your wand at the archway. We only want light, no sparks, is that clear?'

Jack sighed.

'I'll try my best.'

'Now Elan, take the five branches and lay them in order, starting from the other side of the sentinels, oak, beech, willow, birch and lastly the pine.'

Elan laid the branches in between the two trees, making a green carpet on the bare forest floor. Nora passed Elan the acorn and she laid it in the centre of her open palm.

'All is ready,' announced Nora. 'Let us begin.'

Jack pointed his wand and willed the gateway to appear with all his might. Nora whispered some words Jack didn't understand and a soft golden light began to glow from Elan's palm. The harder Jack concentrated the brighter the acorn grew. He tried to keep a steady light at the end of his wand, but his hands were trembling. Without warning it seemed to erupt and a blinding light forced Jack's eyes to close. He blinked then opened them again. Before him rose a pair of tall green doors. They were covered in golden carvings, which gleamed as brightly as the acorn.

'You did it!' cried Camelin. 'You did it!'

'What a welcome sight,' said Nora. 'I'd begun to worry that we might not see Glasruhen Gate again.'

'At last!' sighed Elan. 'Well done Jack, now there really is hope for us all.'

Jack couldn't take his eyes off the doors, which filled the archway between the two Sentinel Oaks. He'd never seen anything like them before.

'What happens now?' he asked.

'We go through into Annwn,' replied Elan.

'We won't be long, we'll be back in a flash so you can wait here for us and then we'll get you back home before 10 o'clock,' fussed Nora. 'I think we'll take your wand with us too Jack, just in case. We don't want any accidents, you really shouldn't use it unsupervised.'

Nora and Elan picked up the cauldron and stepped forward. As Nora passed Jack she paused and waited while he put his wand and her Book of Shadows inside the cauldron, next to Camelin's wand.

'Be good,' she said as they stepped onto the first branch.

A low rumbling noise filled the forest. The two doors parted and a green glow shone through the crack. When they stepped onto the second branch the doorway opened wider, then it creaked loudly, and finally swung open completely. Nora and Elan stepped onto the beech branch then disappeared.

'Where'd they go?' asked Camelin.

'They just vanished.'

Camelin hopped over to the first branch and peered into the greenness. Jack couldn't move. He was still shaking.

'What can you see?'

'Nothing, come on, let's go and have a look, just a quick peek, it won't do any harm.'

Jack wasn't happy.

'We can't, we promised.'

'Now that's where you're wrong, we didn't promise anything.'

'Weren't you listening? It said in the book that we can't enter until Samhain. If we do we're in trouble.'

'I was listening but it didn't say anything about ravens, did it?'

Jack shook his head and tried to protest, but Camelin continued.

'Naw it didn't. And we won't have to walk over the branches we can fly through. What d'you say?'

'Nora will be back soon. We'd better wait here as

she asked us to. What would happen if she came back and found us gone?'

'I want to go to the fair!'

'So do I,' piped a familiar voice.

'And me too,' said Charkle.

'You followed us again,' snapped Camelin.

'Nobody said we couldn't. You were supposed to come and tell us when you were going on another adventure,' Timmery replied. 'Don't forget, we have secrets now.'

Camelin frowned at the little bats.

'Maybe my family went into Annwn, through one of the other gateways before they got closed. I can't rest until I've searched everywhere. I'd like to go and look for them.'

'Come on Jack, we can say we were helping Charkle. You did promise him that when the cauldron was remade we'd help him.'

'I did,' agreed Jack. 'But…'

'No buts, let's transform now. We can leave your clothes here; no one's going to find them. Close your eyes everyone.'

Jack shook his feathers. He still wasn't happy about going through Glasruhen Gate, even as a bird, but the green glow from the gateway did look inviting. And he too wanted to see the fair.

'You promise we won't be long, just a quick look. I told Orin I wouldn't be late tonight.'

'We'll be back before you know it.'

'Won't it be dark in Annwn?' asked Timmery. 'The sun's gone down now.'

'Have a quick look for us and see what's going on. If Nora's still on the other side, she'll see us straight away, but she won't notice you.'

'Ooh! The start of an adventure, I love adventures.'

'I don't think we're going to be gone long enough for it to be an adventure Timmery,' said Jack, but the little bat had already flitted into the green glow.

'That was quick,' said Camelin as Timmery reappeared. 'What's it like? Was Nora there? Did anyone see you?'

'Can't see a thing, there's bright sunlight on the other side.'

'I'll go,' said Charkle. 'I can see in daylight.'

'Couldn't you see anything at all?' asked Camelin after Charkle had gone.

Before Timmery could answer Charkle flitted back through the archway.

'It's safe to go through. I can't see anyone around at all. It's deserted.'

'Deserted?' croaked Camelin. 'What d'you mean deserted? What about the fair?'

'No fair, no people. Just hills and fields.'

'Come on Jack, we need to go and see for ourselves. There has to be a fair.'

Jack hesitated.

'It's alright for the rest of you, but if we get caught I'm the mortal. I'm the one who'll be in trouble.'

'They'd have to catch us first,' laughed Camelin. 'We can fly faster than anyone can run. Coming?'

'I suppose so.'

Timmery fluttered around the gateway.

'What am I going to do? I can't see a thing through there.'

'Then you'll have to stay here, Charkle can keep you company. We'll tell you all about it when we get back,' replied Camelin.

'Or you could climb onto my back,' said Jack. 'But you'd have to hold tight.'

'Oh I will Jack Brenin, I will. Thank you, thank you.'

When Timmery had attached himself to Jack's feathers Camelin hopped forward.

'Ready?'

'Ready,' Timmery and Charkle replied.

'How will we know when it's time to come back?' asked Jack

'When we can't eat anymore,' chuckled Camelin. 'Come on, let's go and find that fair.'

Jack watched as the others disappeared into the glowing green light. He hesitated for a moment before he took off and followed them through Glasruhen Gate.

INTO ANNWN

On the other side of the portal the green glow faded and was immediately replaced by dazzling sunshine. Undulating fields stretched as far as the eye could see to the left and right of a well-trodden pathway. Through the glare Jack could see that the sky was cornflower blue and dotted with slow moving clouds. The path snaked from the portal into the distance and eventually disappeared over the brow of a small hill. The only two trees near the gateway were the Sentinel Oaks. Camelin was perched on one of the lower branches.

'Thought you'd changed your mind.'

'Won't the trees tell Nora what we've done?'

'Naw, that lot in the forest have been sleeping for years and none of the Dryads followed us as far as the gateway.'

'But what about the Sentinels?'

'They haven't stirred for hundreds of years. You'd need really strong magic to wake them.'

Camelin danced around on the branch.

'We're here on official business,' he croaked loudly then stopped and listened. 'See, what'd I tell you, we don't even know their names. They're not going to wake up if we don't address them properly.'

Jack was relieved when the trees didn't stir, he wasn't sure that going to the fair would count as *official business*. He could see Camelin was getting impatient as he hopped from foot to foot.

'Come on we're wasting time. The fair must be near the Citadel and that's got to be at the end of this path.'

'I'm not sure we should go any further, you said we were only going to take a peek. And how do you know the Citadel's that way?'

'Gwillam told me you couldn't get lost in Annwn; all roads lead to the Glass Palace and that's in the middle of the Citadel. Come on.'

Before Jack could reply Camelin took off in the direction of the hill.

'Are you coming Jack?' asked Charkle. 'What harm can it do just to take a look?'

'Oh please Jack, let's go and see now we're here,' piped Timmery.

'I suppose a quick look can't hurt, hold tight.'

As Jack followed the path he had time to look at the fields below. No birds sang and he couldn't see a single person. Maybe they were all at the fair, but there was a strange emptiness. The only sound was their beating wings.

'I don't like this,' Jack shouted to Camelin. 'Why is it all so quiet? Where is everyone?'

Camelin had reached the top of the hill and landed on the grass.

'Aw Jack, come and look at this!'

Jack landed next to him. He was too amazed to speak.

'What is it?' asked Timmery. 'What can you see?'

'You can see for miles,' Jack told him. 'And it's all so beautiful.'

'See, it's just like I said,' croaked Camelin.

'What is?' piped Timmery.

Jack took a deep breath before trying to describe to Timmery the most beautiful place he'd ever seen.

'There's a lake surrounded by great oaks and in the middle is a palace with four glass towers. There's a flag flying from each turret…'

'That's the Citadel,' Camelin interrupted.

'… and behind the palace you can see the mountains…'

'That's where the *Caves of Eternal Rest* can be found,' added Camelin knowledgeably. 'That's where the Druids go.'

Jack sighed.

'Who's telling Timmery, you or me?'

'Carry on please.'

'There are villages, more hills and what looks like a swamp with a great mound and a ring of tall stones around it, like the ones on Glasruhen Hill.'

'But best of all, there's a fair,' said Camelin. 'That's why it was so quiet, the whole of Annwn's there.'

'Those mountains look like the best place to start searching,' said Charkle.

'We'll go and look when we come back at Samhain,' croaked Camelin. 'Right now we have some serious eating to do, I can smell sausages.'

Jack was still worried. He didn't want to leave the hill. They'd had a look and he really thought they ought to go back through the gate.

'If everyone in Annwn's at the fair, won't Nora and Elan be there too? They'll see us and then we'll be in a lot of trouble.'

'Naw, they won't be there, not a chance. See that tree in the distance, the one on its own near the mountains, that's the Mother Oak. Nora and Elan will be there right now collecting Hamadryad acorns.'

'What if they've got them already?'

'You should have asked your Book of Shadows all these questions, we're wasting time. Nora will need to go to the Crochan tree and pick the leaves to make the elixir, that's going to take her a while. Then she'll have to go and present the rhubarb to the King of the Festival.'

'King of the Festival?'

'He's not a real King, there's only a Queen in Annwn. If you're chosen to be the King of the Festival it's only for the day. Any fruit from the other side is given to the King, he passes it on to the cooks and they prepare it for everyone to share at the Festival Feast. We won't be here for that as it doesn't start until sunset. Now, are you coming or not?'

'I'm not,' announced Charkle. 'I'm going to take a look at the mountains.'

'We ought to stick together,' said Jack.

'It won't take me long. I'll probably be back before Camelin's finished eating.'

'Fine,' grumbled Camelin. 'You go, and take Timmery with you if you want.'

'I'm staying with Jack, it's too bright for me. I can't see a thing.'

'We'll meet you on the other side of the portal. There's no point trying to meet up anywhere else. If you're not back in time it's your own fault,' grumbled Camelin.

'See you later,' Charkle called as he flew off towards the mountains.

'So, are you coming?' said Camelin.

Jack nodded.

As they got closer to the ring of trees, they could hear the sound of music and laughter floating on the breeze. Jack could see crowds of people. He looked for Nora and Elan, but luckily they were nowhere to be seen. A large group sat on the grass, gathered around what could only have been a storyteller. At the edge of the lake, small boats bobbed up and down in the water. From the island, the four squat glass towers of the Palace glinted in the sunlight.

Jack saw jugglers and then, coming towards them, two men in brightly coloured robes walking on stilts, their heads almost level with the lower branches of the great oaks. Under each of the trees which surrounded the lake were circular tables; most were piled high with prepared food, like cakes and pies, but the one Camelin was heading towards had an enormous barbecue beside it. A pig roasted over a fire in a pit, there was a great pan full of sweet chestnuts and Jack could smell jacket potatoes. But the most delicious smell of all came from a row of sausages on the grill. Jack followed Camelin. They landed on the branches of the first of the trees above a stall displaying handmade sweets. Camelin hopped excitedly from foot to foot.

'Look at that! All my favourite sweets ... marshmallows, cinder toffee, nougat and fudge. I'm going to sample a bit from here before I make a start on the sausages. What are you waiting for? Come on, let's go and help ourselves.'

Before Jack could speak Camelin was descending towards the sweets. There was a loud cry from one of the women, she grabbed a broom and lashed out. Camelin swerved and returned to the branch with a beak full of fudge.

'What happened?' he managed to croak.

'I think she called you a thief!'

'She did,' confirmed Timmery. 'And she told you to keep your thieving beak off her fudge.'

The disturbance hadn't gone unnoticed. The crowd below were looking up into the branches, trying to see where Camelin had gone.

'You're supposed to be able to help yourself to anything you want here,' he grumbled. 'I've dreamt of this moment for years. This wasn't how I expected it to be. No one ever said anything about being attacked with a broom.'

'I'm not sure it's free. Look over there. It looks like those people are paying money for something.'

'Naw, that can't be right, there's no money in Annwn. Perhaps I should have done my shuffle dance.'

'Maybe we should go. Those people don't look too friendly to me.'

'Trust me, I know what I'm doing. I'll go and entertain that man over there at the barbecue and I'll have a string of sausages back here in no time, you'll see.'

Jack knew Camelin had made up his mind so it was no use trying to dissuade him. The smell of the barbecue wafted up to them on the breeze. Camelin breathed deeply then hopped through the canopy towards the grill.

'Here we go!' he croaked as he swooped down and managed a loop-the-loop before landing gracefully in front of the man cooking sausages. He immediately began twirling and shuffling.

Jack thought the man looked worried as he reached down and threw something, which Camelin caught easily in his beak. He flipped his prize into the air and swallowed it whole, then began to cough and choke.

'Ugh! It's charcoal.'

The man launched two more pieces at Camelin and began waving his arms.

'Plan two,' Camelin croaked as he took off towards the barbecue. He swooped past the grill and helped himself to a string of cooked sausages. He struggled to gain height, but eventually made the safety of the branches with his prize.

The man shouted angrily and pointed to the tree and a crowd began to gather. Camelin didn't seem too bothered.

'Supper!' he cried triumphantly. 'D'you want some?'

'No thank you,' said Jack and Timmery together.

Jack felt very uneasy. The dense canopy shielded them from the group of people below but this didn't feel like the beautiful, peaceful place he'd been told about. Something was wrong. It was time they went home.

'I think we ought to go back through the portal now.'

'Whatever for? These are great, you ought to try one.'

'We shouldn't have come.'

'But we've only just got here. We haven't been round the fair yet.'

'I don't think any of those people down there are going to let us go round the fair.'

Camelin finished the last sausage and looked down, at what was now an angry looking crowd.

'Maybe you're right. We came and had a look. I don't want any more lumps of charcoal thrown at me.'

Jack felt a lot happier once they'd flown over the small hill above the village. He'd looked back a couple of times. There was no sign of Charkle, but more importantly, no one had followed them. There was only a short distance left before they reached Glasruhen Gate.

'It'll be different next time we come, we'll be with Nora and Elan, they won't throw charcoal at you then, we'll be guests.'

'It was worth it, those sausages really were the best I've ever tasted. You'll have to have some at Samhain. It's a shame we didn't get a chance to sample the pies.'

Jack laughed. He wondered if Charkle was already waiting for them on the other side of the portal. The open doors of Glasruhen Gate were just ahead. He could see the green light coming from the archway.

'Ready?' Camelin called as they approached the Sentinel Oaks.

Jack didn't get a chance to reply. He saw Camelin stop in mid flight, his wings continued to flap but he wasn't moving. Seconds later Jack stopped too. He struggled to free himself from the invisible barrier they'd both flown into. Two men leapt out from behind the doors.

'We've got 'em Jed, nabbed 'em good and proper.'

'Sure 'ave, Teg, let's get 'em back to the Citadel. His Lordship's not going to be too pleased the Western Gate's been opened.'

Struggling was pointless, they were tangled in a fine silver net, which had been strung between the Sentinel Oaks. Camelin shook his head and made a low ssshh'ing sound, which Jack presumed meant he wasn't to speak. Neither of them struggled as the two men unhooked the net, they were too entangled to escape. The men tied the ends together and made a loop, pushed a large pole through the hole, then hoisted it onto their shoulders and set off towards the Citadel.

'You wouldn't think a couple of birds could weigh so much would ya?' said Jed as they struggled up the hillside.

'Heaviest ones we've ever caught. His Lordship isn't going to be pleased they got in,' replied Teg.

There was a lot of puffing and blowing as Jed and Teg struggled to the top of the hill. They put the pole down whilst they got their breath back.

Jack wondered if Camelin had a plan. They might get a chance to escape once the net was removed. He'd already tried pecking it to see if he could make a hole, but the silver thread wouldn't break. He didn't think it was a good idea to talk. Maybe if *His Lordship*, whoever he was, thought they were just a couple of stray birds who'd flown in through the portal they might not be in so much trouble. It was then Jack really started to worry. What if they found out he'd opened Glasruhen Gate? It was obviously something *His Lordship* wasn't going to be pleased about.

Teg and Jed once more hoisted the pole onto their shoulders. Jack felt sick as the net they were suspended in swung from side to side. He could hear voices now as they neared the circle of oak trees by the water's edge. As they passed a group of people the chattering and laughing stopped. First there was silence then whispering began.

'Stop!' shrieked one of the women as Jed and Teg passed by. 'That's the thief what took my fudge.'

'And there's the one who stole my sausages,' the man from the barbecue shouted.

Jed stopped and removed a slate from his pocket. Teg handed him a pencil.

'If you two would like to make a statement I'll pass it on to the Captain of the Guard. We'll be reporting to him as soon as we get across to the Citadel.'

The woman from the sweet stall didn't waste any

time telling Jed all about the incident. Then the man from the barbecue stepped forward.

'Make sure you put down that it was a whole string of my best sausages he stole.'

'Best sausages, whole string,' Jed said as he wrote.

Jack was wondering how the people knew they were the same birds they'd seen earlier. Then Camelin burped and everyone looked round. Now they really were in trouble. Was it a serious crime if a bird took food? Birds on Earth took any food they could find, all the time. Jack wondered what they did with ravens in Annwn.

Jed and Teg continued to the edge of the lake where a small boat was tethered. Teg clambered in.

'Pass 'em over.'

Jed didn't seem to care if Jack and Camelin got bumped against the seats as he passed them in.

It was uncomfortable in the boat. They'd been tossed into the bottom where a puddle of water washed over them each time the boat rocked from side to side.

Jack was glad when they reached the other side and the swaying stopped. Once more the men hoisted the pole onto their shoulders. But instead of going up to the Citadel they began to descend a flight of steps which had been carved into the rock face. The steps led from the quay to a large door. Jed rapped on the door with the end of the pole and shouted loudly: 'Prisoners for the dungeon.'

Jack gulped. They really were in a lot of trouble.

DEEP TROUBLE

'In here,' ordered the guard who'd opened the outer door.

Jed and Teg slid the silver net off the pole onto the floor of the dungeon. Jack and Camelin landed in a heap on the stone flags. The light dimmed as the guards withdrew and the door slammed shut. A tiny grill in the door let in a glimmer of light from the burning torch on the corridor wall. The sound of footsteps walking back down the passage was followed by silence.

'Is everyone OK?' asked Jack.

'Squashed, battered, bruised and soggy,' grumbled Camelin.

'I'm fine, just a bit tangled,' piped Timmery.

'What do we do now?' continued Jack.

'If I wriggle out I can go and have a look around,' suggested Timmery. 'I can find out where everything is and see if we can work out how to escape.'

'I thought you couldn't see anything?' grumbled Camelin.

'That was outside. I'm fine in here in the dark.'

Jack and Camelin lay still until Timmery managed to untangle himself and squeeze through one of the holes in the net.

'Back soon,' he said cheerfully before flitting through the grill in the door.

'Let's try to get out of the net,' suggested Camelin. 'I've been trying to peck a hole in it since they caught us but I've not had any luck.'

'I've had a go too. It must be made of something really strong. Do you think there's enough room for me to transform in the net? I might be able to untie the loops then.'

Camelin had a shuffle around as best he could.

'Great idea Jack, I'm sure there's enough room.'

As they touched foreheads the whole dungeon lit up. By the time Jack was able to see again the light had gone. He'd expected to feel squashed by the netting but he wasn't. He reached out to find the loop but nothing happened. He didn't have hands as he'd expected, he still had feathers and wings.

'Something's wrong, I've not changed.'

'Something's very wrong. I'm naked!'

'How can that be? You mean you're a boy!'

'I'm a boy! After all these years I've got arms and legs again. I'm a boy!'

'How?'

'I don't know, it must be something to do with us being in Annwn. On Earth you're a boy and I'm a raven, here it's the other way round. Nora said I could be a boy again in Annwn but I thought she meant there was some kind of magic that could transform me. I never thought it would happen like this.'

'Can you untie the loop?'

'I'll try.'

Camelin fumbled with the net for a long time. Eventually he managed to undo the knot. He wriggled out and held the net open for Jack to get free. Once Jack had shaken his feathers Camelin began hopping around the cell.

'I'm a real boy! Look I can walk!'

'Do you think we'd better transform back again in case someone comes?'

'Naw, not yet, I've waited a long time to have legs

again, just a bit longer won't hurt. It feels so good.'

Jack sighed. He couldn't help feeling worried.

'Let's hope Timmery comes back with some good news. If we can get out of here we'll fly as fast as we can to Glasruhen Gate.'

'What if they've got another net waiting?'

'When we got caught you could see the net didn't reach up to the top of the arch, that's where we'll aim for. It'll be like flying through the window in time again. We know we can get through a small space with our wings tucked in.'

Jack was impressed that Camelin had already worked out a plan of escape.

'I'm not looking forward to hearing what Nora's going to say.'

'D'you think we could get back without her finding out?'

'I doubt it, do you?'

'Naw, you're right, we're going to be in big trouble. I'm sorry I got you into all this. I promise I'll never take any food again, even if it's supposed to be free. Nora won't be mad with you. I'll tell her it was all my fault. You know she'll believe me.'

'It's not all your fault. I didn't have to come into Annwn. The truth is, I wanted to but I was afraid and didn't want to get into trouble.'

'At least they don't know who we are. Did you hear the guards? They just think two birds have got into Annwn.'

'Who do you think *His Lordship* is?'

'No idea.'

'Didn't Gwillam or Nora ever mention him?'

'Naw, they told me about the Blessed Council but not about any Lords. I told you, Annwn's got a Queen.'

'What's she like?'

'I don't know, but Gwillam told me she had three heads.'

'Three heads!'

'Yeh, kind of scary don't you think? I've never seen anything with three heads before.'

Jack wasn't sure he needed to meet the Queen of Annwn.

'I thought she was called Queen of the Fair Folk?'

'She is.'

'Does that mean all the Fair Folk have three heads?'

Before Jack got his answer Timmery flew back through the grill.

'Who're you?' he squeaked.

'It's me, Camelin.'

'But you're a boy!'

'I know isn't it great? Look!'

Camelin did a human version of his shuffle dance in the cell. Jack could only make out the shape of the dance but he had a good idea what Camelin was doing.

'You're naked,' said Timmery.

Camelin stopped dancing and promptly sat down.

'I know but nobody can see.'

'I can, I see really well in the dark.'

'I think it's time we transformed back again Jack, hide your eyes Timmery.'

Jack and Camelin touched foreheads. There was no bright light.

'Can I look now?'

'Naw, we've got to try again.'

Once more they held their foreheads together, a little longer this time but still nothing happened.

'What's wrong?' asked Timmery.

'We've got a big problem. I'm stuck, I can't transform back. Even if we could escape I'm not going to be able to fly through the arch at the top of Glasruhen Gate now.'

'Don't worry we'll find a way to get out. When

it's dark Timmery can go and look for Nora, she'll get us out of here.'

'That's if Timmery can get out.'

'Oh I think I can. I've had a look around. The only door to the outside is the one we came through and that's solid but they have to change the guard sometime. I can hide in the back of his hood when he goes through the door. We just have to wait.'

Camelin began gathering the net together.

'Have you got a plan too?' asked Timmery.

'Naw, I thought I'd try and use the net. I don't want anyone to see me naked.'

'But it's got holes in it. Why don't you use the sacks at the back of the room? They'd be better.'

'I can't see any sacks.'

'I can. Start walking away from the door towards the other wall... a bit to the left... a bit more, now stop, bend down.'

Camelin followed Timmery's instructions and found the sacks.

'There are some candles here too but they're going to be about as much use as a hot ice cube.'

Camelin ripped a hole in the top of one of the sacks and made two more at the sides then slipped it over his head.

'It's itchy!'

'Better than being naked,' said Jack and Timmery together.

'Sssh!' said Jack. 'Listen!'

There were footsteps coming back down the corridor. A face appeared at the grill then the key turned and the door opened a crack. Two dishes appeared before the door slammed shut and was locked again.

'Aw great, they've fed us. I didn't think we'd get anything to eat.'

'What we got?'

'A dish of water and… you're not going to believe it… birdseed!'

Jack laughed.

'It's not funny, stale bread would have been better.'

'How long do you think Nora and Elan will be in Annwn?'

'Why?'

'Well what if Nora goes back through the gate and can't find us?'

'That wouldn't be good. We need another plan and quick.'

'Charkle could help, he can see in the light,' suggested Timmery.

'But we don't know where he is and he has no idea where we are,' said Camelin.

'Not unless we send him some kind of a signal. He's got to fly back over the Citadel soon. How about the call of the raven-owl? He'll know we're in trouble if he hears it.'

Camelin groaned.

'Is that your best idea? He'll never hear it though all this rock.'

'Oh he will, he will,' said Timmery excitedly. 'Dragonettes have amazing hearing and since he's been transformed into a bat it's even better than it was before.'

'We could try,' said Jack.

'Well it won't do any harm to give it a go I suppose,' agreed Camelin.

Jack threw his head back and started to hoot, Camelin joined in but it wasn't as good as his usual call. Timmery added his own version which was more of a high-pitched squeak. Again and again they called until a banging on the door made them stop.

'Keep the noise down,' the guard shouted as he unlocked the door.

Timmery flitted up to the roof, Camelin tried to hide in the corner and Jack stood still in the centre of the room.

'Out of your net are you? Not eaten your dinner?'

The guard thrust the lighted torch he was carrying into the room then froze. He struggled to speak: 'What... what are you doing in here? Where's the other bird gone? This is going to have to be reported. Looks like we've caught ourselves a shape-shifting spy as well as a thieving raven. His Lordship will be pleased.'

The door slammed once more and darkness returned.

'Now's your chance Timmery, if the guards are going to the Citadel you'll be able to get out,' whispered Jack.

There was no answer from the little bat.

'Timmery?' called Camelin.

'I think he must have gone. Let's hope we get some help soon.'

They sat in a silence broken only by the sound of bird food being stirred around the bowl by Camelin.

Jack woke with a start. The loud snoring coming from the dark shape by his side told him Camelin was asleep. He'd no idea what time it was or how long they'd been in the cell. He wondered where Timmery was and if help was on its way. There wasn't any point in waking Camelin; probably the best thing he could do was to try and sleep again. He shut his eyes then thought he heard someone calling his name. He listened hard and there it was again.

'Jack, Jack.'

This time it was closer.

'Camelin, where are you?'

'Charkle!' cried Jack, 'in here.'

A tiny bat with a long tail flitted in through the bars.

'I've been looking everywhere for you.'

'How did you get in?'

'Let's have some light in here first,' said Charkle as he breathed a small flame, which promptly went out when he saw Camelin.

'Who's that? Where's Camelin?'

'I am Camelin.'

'But...'

'I know, I'm a boy. We haven't got time to go through all that; tell us what you know and how you got in. And more importantly, can we get out?'

'Wait a minute,' said Jack. 'Didn't you find a candle near those sacks? At least we'll be able to have a bit of light now.'

Charkle's flame gave Camelin enough light to find
the candle again. When it was lit they sat around it.

'So, can we get out?'

'Not without help. I knew you were in trouble
when I heard the call but I didn't imagine you were
in this kind of trouble. How did you end up in the
dungeon in the first place?'

Camelin coughed.

'It's a long story and we haven't got time now. Can
you get out again and go and find Nora?'

'I'll go and wait by the door. I got in when
someone went out. It's bound to be opened again
sometime soon.'

'Did you see Timmery?' asked Jack.

'No, but I wasn't looking for him.'

'Find Nora, tell her where we are and beg her to
come and get us out of here,' said Camelin.

'Where should I go and look?'

Camelin spread out one of the sacks and started
sprinkling birdseed on it until he'd outlined some of the
places they'd seen from the hill. He pointed to one of the
piles of seed. Charkle sat on his shoulder and watched.

'Do you remember that tree near the
mountains?'

'The Mother Oak?'

'Yes, that's where Nora and Elan were going first. When they've been there and collected the acorns they'll go and see Gwillam, over here by the Northern Gateway.'

'How do you know she'll go to Gwillam's? She's got to go to the Crochan tree hasn't she?' interrupted Jack.

'The Crochan tree is in Gwillam's garden and even if she didn't have to get the acorns she'd go and see him anyway. He is her brother after all.'

'Brother?' said Jack and Charkle together.

'I haven't got time to explain family trees now, we've got far more important things to worry about. Now, do you think you can find them?'

'I hope so, I'm sure Nora will have you out of here in no time. I'll be back with help as soon as I can.'

Charkle flitted through the grill in the door and was gone.

'What now?' asked Jack.

'We wait.'

'I'm getting hungry.'

'Me too, but I'm not eating birdseed. Go ahead if you want some.'

Jack shook his head. He wondered how long it would be before help arrived.

The creaking of a door in the distance broke the silence inside the dungeon. Jack and Camelin strained to listen for footsteps. A key turned in a lock a long way off.

'Do you think Charkle got out?' asked Jack.

'Oh he did, he did,' an excited voice said from the other side of the grill.

Timmery flittered into the cell.

'We didn't get chance to say anything but I saw him and he saw me. Is he going to get help?'

'We hope so,' said Jack.

'Why've you come back,' asked Camelin.

'I had to, I thought you'd want to know what was going on. It's not good, not good at all.'

'Oh thank you,' grumbled Camelin.

'Never mind him, just tell us what you found out.'

Timmery fluttered around their heads. Jack could see something had upset him.

'You're in deep trouble, both of you. The guard went up to the Citadel and got taken to a big chamber.

140

This important looking man came in, the guard bowed and I nearly fell out of his hood…'

'Never mind the details, just tell us the important stuff. How much trouble are we in?' asked Camelin.

'I'm coming to that. The guard called the man *Sire*. I thought you only called a king Sire?'

'You do,' agreed Jack.

'Well who was he?' asked Camelin.

'His name is Velindur.'

Camelin looked puzzled.

'Annwn's never had a king, something's not right.'

'He's the one who's in charge,' continued Timmery. 'He was furious when the guard told him one of the ravens in the dungeon was now a boy. He shouted, called you a shape-shifting spy and said you'd have to be interrogated.'

'What about me?' asked Jack, 'what did he say about the other raven?'

'They think you stole the food; he said you were a thief and would have to be tried. He's going to call the Blessed Council together. He said they'd decide how you're both going to be punished.'

'This isn't good,' sighed Camelin. 'We really are in deep trouble. If we've got to stand trial Nora won't be

141

able to do anything. The Blessed Council will decide our fate. It'll be even worse when they find out we came through Glasruhen Gate…'

'… and uninvited too,' added Jack. 'They'll say we've trespassed, won't they?'

'They will.'

'What will they do to us?'

'I don't know, but I'm not in any hurry to find out.'

INTERROGATION

'What's that?' asked Timmery as a low rumbling noise made him jump.

'Camelin,' explained Jack.

Timmery looked at Camelin.

'Sorry, it's that piece of charcoal. It's really upset my stomach.'

'You don't think it might have anything to do with the piece of fudge and seven sausages you ate?' enquired Timmery.

'How d'you know it was seven sausages?'

'Jack told me.'

'Thanks Jack.'

They sat in silence except for the occasional

rumbling of Camelin's stomach. A jangling of keys gave them a start.

'On yer feet, nice an easy, don't want no trouble,' the guard said as he unlocked the door.

Jack could see Jed and Teg behind their jailor.

'Ready with the net Teg?'

'Ready.'

Teg jumped into the room holding what looked like a large fishing net. The guard held the flaming torch towards Camelin while Teg netted Jack.

'Hold yer hands out boy,' said Jed.

Camelin did as he was told. Cold iron bracelets were clamped shut on both wrists. Jed tugged at a chain attached to each cuff and pulled Camelin towards the door.

'His Lordship wants to interrogate you.'

The guard pointed at Jack.

'The bird too?'

'Yep, the bird too. He said bring both the prisoners an' we does as we're told.'

Jack didn't feel good. He heard a great gurgle coming from Camelin's stomach. He didn't think it was the charcoal this time. Teg grabbed one of the sacks, tipped the net upside down and shook Jack into it. He quickly tied the top then slung it over his shoulder.

Camelin was right, it was itchy inside the sack but at least Jack managed to peck a hole in the bottom so he could see out. He wondered about trying to escape as they made their way up the rock staircase, but he couldn't leave Camelin on his own. He knew he'd broken the Law of Annwn and would have to face up to what he'd done. He wished he'd asked his Book of Shadows more questions about the law, but it wasn't something he'd been planning to break.

By the time they entered the Glass Palace Jack felt seasick. He wished all the bouncing up and down would stop. It did, abruptly, when Teg came to a halt before two great golden doors. A guard, dressed in a yellow and red uniform stepped forward.

'Prisoners for King Velindur,' announced Teg.

The great doors swung open and Jack could see a beautiful chamber. Its circular walls were made of glass; they must be in one of the towers. A stern looking man sat on a throne towards the back of the room. His dark hair flowed past his shoulders and his thick eyebrows almost met in the middle. He looked neither old nor young. Jack didn't think he looked very pleased to see Jed and Teg.

'Enter,' he commanded. 'Put the prisoners in the cage and leave.'

Teg and Jed bowed low and then quickly made their way to a silver cage at the far end of the room. The cage looked big enough for a man to stand up in. As they opened the door a guard stepped towards the glass wall and drew a long curtain. Jed pushed Camelin inside and Teg threw the sack in after him. Jack landed with a thud on the stone floor. Camelin quickly bent over and untied the sack.

'That will be all,' the man told the guard.

It was the first time Jack had seen Camelin properly. It felt strange seeing someone he knew in a different body. If they'd been standing next to each other as boys, Camelin would have been a good head taller than Jack. His hair was very dark and thick. He looked more like a street urchin than a Druid's acolyte, his long arms and legs were very grubby and the sack didn't fit too well. Jack wondered if Camelin felt strange being a boy again as Jack had felt strange the first time he'd changed into a raven. His thoughts were interrupted when the man left the throne and circled around the cage. Was this King Velindur or one

146

of the Blessed Council? Jack got his answer when the man spoke to Camelin.

'I expect my subjects to bow before their King.'

Neither of them replied. Camelin stood with his mouth open.

'No matter, there's no place for anyone who spies or thieves in Annwn. You will both stand trial before the Blessed Council, they can decide your fate. But in the meantime, I'd like some answers.'

Velindur held up his hand and counted off the questions on his fingers, one by one, as he spoke.

'Who are you? How did you open the Western Portal? Who sent you? Why did you come into Annwn? I'm going to leave you to think about those questions and when I return I will have your answers. Understood?'

Camelin nodded. Jack thought it was best to pretend he hadn't understood any of the conversation. King Velindur turned and strode away. He passed through a smaller door that led into another chamber. As soon as he'd gone Jack heard the fluttering of wings above the cage, more than one pair of wings.

Timmery said: 'Don't look up and don't say anything, just in case anyone's watching. Charkle's got some news.'

'I was waiting by the dungeon door so I could

get back in to tell you the good news. When the door opened you were coming out so I followed you here.'

Jack watched Camelin frown. He too wished Charkle would hurry up and tell them the news.

'I found Nora at Gwillam's house. I've told her everything and she says not to worry. But you must answer every question truthfully, and if possible, Jack's not to say anything at all. The longer Velindur thinks he's just a raven the better. Camelin, you must tell him you're Gwillam's acolyte, and then they'll have a better chance of getting you out of here. I'm taking Timmery back with me to Gwillam's house; Nora's got plans for us. Don't worry. Just remember to tell the truth.'

Camelin let out a big sigh. The two little bats flittered towards the doorway and attached themselves to one of the tall columns by the golden doors. They didn't have long to wait. A loud knock brought Velindur out of the side chamber and back to his throne. Once he was seated he commanded the doors to be opened. A servant entered carrying something on a silver tray, followed by another carrying a small table. The table was placed before the throne and a delicious smelling apple pie was presented to the King. Jack had been watching the servants, so he hadn't noticed Charkle or Timmery leave. He hoped no one else had either.

Velindur ate the whole pie. Jack and Camelin watched every mouthful disappear. A low rumbling sound came from Jack's stomach. He realised he was hungry. He'd not eaten since they'd come through the portal.

When he'd finished Velindur paced up and down the room.

'Now for some answers. Who are you?'

Camelin gulped and tried to speak, his throat was dry and his voice came out as a hoarse whisper: 'I'm Camelin, acolyte to Gwillam, High Druid and Keeper of the Shrine in the Sacred Grove by the Holy Oak Well.'

'You lie. Gwillam does not have an acolyte, neither is he the keeper of any shrines or holy wells.'

'I'm Gwillam's acolyte,' Camelin announced again more forcefully than before.

'How did you open the Western Portal?'

'I didn't.'

'Again, I say you lie. How else could you have come through Glasruhen Gate into Annwn?'

'The gate was already open when I came through.'

Jack could see Velindur was getting angry.

'Who sent you?' he shouted and banged his fist on the bars.

'No one sent me. I came because I wanted to.'

'Why?'

'Because I wanted to go to the fair.'

'That's the worst pack of lies I've ever heard from anyone. I say you are a shape-shifting spy. Try to deny that.'

'I can't shape-shift and I'm not a spy.'

Velindur's face turned red and he glowered through the bars at Camelin. Jack tried not to take any notice, but he jumped when Velindur's fist hit the cage again.

'GUARD!'

The golden doors swung open and one of the guards stepped in and bowed.

'Fetch Tegfryn and Jedwyn. NOW!'

The guard left hurriedly and returned shortly with Jed and Teg.

'Take this prisoner back to the dungeon. He is to have no food or water. The Blessed Council have been summoned. He can come before them when they've assembled. I don't care if he rots in his cell, understood? When you've done that come back, I've got a job for you both.'

Jed and Teg fumbled with the key before they managed to unlock the cage and tug Camelin out. They walked him backwards to the door, bowing as they went. Teg thrust Camelin's head down and made him bow too.

Once they'd gone Velindur paced up and down the room, muttering to himself. Jack wondered if the two guards were coming back for him. If he wasn't going back to the dungeon, what were they going to do with him? Did they eat ravens in Annwn?

Velindur seemed preoccupied. Jack hoped he'd forget about him altogether.

When they returned, Jed and Teg stood nervously before Velindur. Jack could see he wasn't pleased.

'Who came through the Western Portal?'

Jed and Teg looked at each other.

'It's a simple question,' growled Velindur. 'Who came into Annwn?'

'The prisoners Sire,' replied Teg.

'Anyone else?'

'No Sire.'

'Who opened the gate?'

'It opened on its own Sire,' said Jed nervously.

'Portal Gates don't just open on their own. Did you see the boy open the doors?'

The two guards shook their heads.

'It was open when we got there so we got the net out Sire,' explained Teg.

'I've a good mind to have you two thrown into the dungeon with the spy. I'm surrounded by idiots.'

Jed and Teg looked at their feet. Jack wondered why they hadn't seen Nora and Elan come through the portal, but no one had been around when they'd flown through. Maybe they'd been having a nap somewhere?

'We have a problem,' began Velindur as he paced up and down the room. 'There may be more intruders in Annwn. I've sent guards to the gates. You must not tell anyone the Western Portal's been opened. I want you to search for intruders. Find out if anyone has seen anything suspicious or unusual. Don't arrest anyone, but make sure you report back to me before sunset. Understood?'

Jed and Teg bobbed up and down again as they backed out of the room. Jack breathed a sigh of relief. Velindur obviously didn't know about Nora and Elan. He wished Nora would come and rescue them soon. He shuddered when he thought about Camelin being back in the dungeon. He hoped he was alright. Jack stayed very still. He didn't want to draw attention to himself. Velindur went over to a large full-length mirror and adjusted his robe before he began muttering to himself again.

'The cauldron must have been remade, it's the only explanation. The acolyte used it to open the portal and was on his way to Gwillam. It's a plot. He's got something Gwillam needs to overthrow me. Well it's not going to happen. I've got to get rid of Gwillam. Yes, that's the answer. He's the one the Blessed Council listens to. If he were out of the way, they'd listen to me. I need to prove Gwillam's acolyte was spying and get evidence that the pair of them were plotting, then I could get rid of them both. The boy must be lying. Why did he choose a raven as a disguise? Didn't he know they'd been banned from Annwn?'

Velindur chuckled to himself then continued thinking aloud.

'Convicting the raven will be easy. After all, he's broken more than one law.'

Jack gulped, Velindur hadn't forgotten about him. None of what he'd heard was good. Maybe he ought to start thinking of a way to escape. He needed to warn Nora and Gwillam. He looked around the room in vain, there was no sign of Timmery or Charkle. Velindur had gone back to his throne and was deep in thought when a gentle tap on the door made him sit bolt upright.

'Enter!'

An old man with wispy grey hair and a kind face strode into the room. In his hand was a long staff made from a branch with an assortment of things tied to it. A bunch of leaves hung from the top and a small bag dangled from a natural hook in the middle. He reminded Jack of someone he knew but he couldn't think who. Velindur didn't look pleased to see his visitor who neither bowed nor called him *Sire*.

'I've received a summons to attend a meeting of the Blessed Council. Is there a problem?'

'There is. My guards have caught two intruders. One is claiming to be your acolyte.'

'That would be Camelin,' the old man said, then laughed. 'What's he been up to?'

Jack realised why the old man looked familiar. It had to be Gwillam, he'd got the same smile as Nora. Velindur didn't speak for a moment.

'Your acolyte is under arrest for trespass, spying, shape-shifting, illegal entry and bringing a forbidden bird into Annwn.'

Gwillam looked around.

'I'm sure there must have been some mistake. Can I see him?'

'No you cannot. When the rest of the Blessed Council get here he can stand before them along with that raven, which is also on a charge of theft and trespass.'

'My acolyte's only a boy.'

'He broke the law.'

'So be it. We'll meet again in the Council Chamber once everyone is here.'

Gwillam turned his back on Velindur and walked to the golden doors. He didn't look back or bow. When he'd gone Velindur stood up and marched out of the room, slamming the door behind him.

Jack had no idea how long he was alone. There didn't seem to be any clocks in Annwn so it was difficult to know what time of day it was. The sun streamed in through the glass walls. He was grateful the curtain had been closed behind the cage. He was dozing when a loud rapping on the golden doors made him jump. Velindur appeared from the small room dressed in a flowing scarlet robe. His trousers looked as if they were made of pure gold. On his feet he wore a pair of heeled shoes, and on his head a jewelled golden crown encrusted with emeralds and rubies. He admired himself in the mirror before collecting a golden staff. He sat on the throne and arranged his robes carefully before calling for whoever had knocked to come in.

Jed and Teg shuffled forward bowing low when they reached the foot of the throne.

'What news?'

'None Sire, no one's seen or heard anything,' said Teg.

'The only intruders anyone knows about are the birds,' added Jed.

'Keep searching and watch Gwillam. I'm sure he's hiding something. See where he goes, what he does and who he speaks to. I know there's something going on, and I'm holding you two responsible for finding out what it is. Understood?'

Jed and Teg nodded.

A guard carried in a small silver tray, upon which lay a large key. Velindur picked it up.

'The Blessed Council have assembled?'

'They have Sire. They await you in the Assembly Room.'

Velindur strode past Jed and Teg.

'Bring the prisoners to the Council Chamber. Both of them,' he commanded as he left the room.

'I'll grab the bird, you get the boy,' said Jed. 'Don't be long, you know His Lordship doesn't like to be kept waiting.'

Once more Jack was put in the sack. He was hustled past a crowd of cloaked and hooded figures who stood in small groups talking quietly to each other. He tried to hear what they were saying but Jed was moving too quickly.

'Make way, make way. Prisoner for the dock, make way,' Jed shouted as he squeezed past the tall figures.

Jack could hear Teg in the background also shouting for the crowd to stand aside. Jack tried to peek at Camelin to see if he was alright but he couldn't see much. The crowd went quiet. Jack heard a pair of heeled shoes pass and then a key turning in a lock.

By the time Jack was released from the sack, the hooded figures had made their way to a semi-circular table and taken their places behind high-backed chairs In front of the table was a rail, behind which was a raised platform. Velindur climbed the steps and seated himself on an ornate throne. Jack and Camelin were thrust inside another cage on the floor beside the platform. The tallest figure spoke. Jack recognised Gwillam's voice.

'The Blessed Council stand before you. Why have we been summoned?'

Velindur stood and pointed towards Jack and Camelin: 'We have intruders, unwelcome guests, trespassers. The boy is a shape-shifting spy, the raven a thief. They have broken the Law of Annwn and must be punished.'

The Blessed Council sat down. Each member wrote on a small slate which was then passed to Gwillam. When all the slates were before him, Gwillam rose once more.

'We all agree. The prisoners must stand trial.'

Velindur smiled but Gwillam hadn't finished.

'The trial will take place at sunset tomorrow.'

'The trial must take place now.'

'The prisoners need time to find a delegate. That is the law.'

Velindur glowered at Gwillam.

'I say we should try them now.'

'The law says they have a day to find someone to represent them. The trial will be tomorrow.'

There was a murmur of agreement from the Blessed Council. Velindur sat down and banged his golden staff three times on the platform. When he had everyone's attention he turned again to Gwillam.

'Then tomorrow it will be. Guards, take the prisoners back to the dungeon.'

Jack's heart sank. He'd hoped the Blessed Council would forgive them and let them go free. He wanted to tell them all how sorry he was, that they hadn't meant any harm. His body started to tremble. He didn't want to go back to the dungeon, but Jed and Teg were already opening the cage door.

'Wait,' cried Gwillam. 'The boy is my acolyte, I take responsibility for him and the raven too. Let me take them home with me. You have my word that I'll bring them back tomorrow night.'

The members of the Blessed Council slowly nodded in agreement. Jack expected Velindur to be annoyed and to shout but instead he appeared to be smiling. He also agreed. Instead of being dragged off to the dungeon, Camelin had his iron cuffs removed and the cage door was opened wide. Camelin ran over to Gwillam, threw his arms around his waist and sobbed. Jack hopped out of the cage. Gwillam held out his arm and he flew onto it.

'Come on,' said Gwillam. 'It's time to go home.'

HOUSE ARREST

Jack hadn't realised how hot and stuffy the Council Chamber had been until the fresh air wafted through his feathers. Freedom had never felt so good. Camelin didn't say anything to Gwillam until they got to the water's edge.

'I'm really very sorry, but you told me that when I got into Annwn I'd be able to eat as much as I wanted.'

Gwillam laughed.

'Not to worry. We'll soon sort this out, you'll see.'

Jack hopped up to Gwillam's shoulder and whispered in his ear.

'We're being watched, it's not safe to talk.'

Gwillam didn't seem too bothered. He shouted to the only boatman standing by the boats: 'We need to cross the water.'

The boatman held out his hand for payment. Gwillam placed a large coin in his palm.

Once they were settled in the boat, Jack hopped onto the prow. He spotted Jed and Teg rowing as fast as they could from the dungeon side of the lake. He wasn't sure if Camelin had seen them too but he didn't want to speak in front of the boatman.

Gwillam winked at Jack then turned to Camelin.

'Was it really seven sausages you ate?'

Camelin hung his head.

'I had a large piece of fudge and a lump of charcoal too.'

'Charcoal! What on earth made you eat charcoal?'

'It wasn't by choice, it was an accident.'

'This is really important. Did you steal anything Jack?'

Jack coughed and pointed his beak towards the boatman. He'd already told Gwillam it wasn't safe to talk. The boatman smiled at Jack.

'I'm Gavin and I'm at your service.'

Jack still didn't say anything. Nora had told him

not to speak. If they thought he was a raven he might be safe. Camelin looked shocked.

'Gavin? Is it really you?'

'I didn't think you'd remember me, it's been so long.'

'You were Gwillam's acolyte before me. Didn't you go to one of the Groves near the Borderlands?'

Gavin nodded.

'What a memory!' exclaimed Gwillam and patted Camelin on the back before turning to Jack. 'You can speak safely on the lake. Gavin is one of us; he's no spy and has no allegiance to Velindur.'

Jack let out a sigh. It hadn't been easy keeping quiet, especially inside the Council Chamber.

'But what about Jed and Teg?' he whispered.

'I don't condone this but sometimes a little bit of magic is necessary. We don't want them catching up with us, do we?'

Gwillam bent his long staff towards the boat behind. Jack didn't see any sparks, but he felt the air shudder. Gwillam smiled.

'That should buy us a bit of time. I hope they can swim!'

Jack thought the little boat looked lower in the water. It began to sink, faster and faster until Jed and Teg were left flapping their arms around and shouting for help. Gwillam flicked his staff again and two oars popped up out of the water. Jed grabbed one and Teg the other. They each hung on with one hand and tried to attract some attention by waving the other. Jack doubted their cries would be heard until the noise from the fair died down. They might be in the water quite a while if they weren't able to get themselves back to the shallows.

'Now where were we? Oh yes, did you eat any of the stolen food Jack?'

'I haven't had anything to eat at all since we came into Annwn.'

'That's excellent, most excellent, couldn't be better.'

Jack couldn't see why not having eaten was a good thing. His stomach was rumbling and all he could think about was food. Camelin's stomach growled too.

'If I'm hungry, Jack must be starving. It's hungry work being a raven, but nobody ever listens to me.'

'It is,' agreed Jack.

'You can eat once we get back. I'm afraid you'll be under house arrest so you're not going to able to go very far, only to the end of my garden and back. I'm responsible for you until the trial, so don't go letting me down.'

'We won't,' said Jack.

'You mean you're going to take us back? I thought you'd rescued us so we could go back through Glasruhen Gate. I didn't think you were really going to make us stand trial. Can't you say we escaped?'

'No Camelin, I can't. You've both broken the law so there must be a trial, but ever since Charkle arrived we've been trying to work out a way to save you.'

'What happens if you can't,' whispered Camelin.

'We'll cross that bridge when we come to it.'

'Is Nora very angry with me?'

'Very angry, she's got a punishment waiting for you when we get back.'

Camelin groaned. Jack shuffled from one foot to the other. He didn't want Camelin to take all the blame.

'It was my fault too. I could have said no and stayed behind.'

'No matter, you can tell Nora everything when we get back. The last, and most important question of all, did you answer all Velindur's questions truthfully?'

'I did.'

'And you Jack?'

'He didn't ask me any questions; he didn't speak to me at all. I'm sure he thinks I'm just an ordinary raven. I heard him talking to himself in his chamber. He's going to try to get you into trouble too, that's why he's told Jed and Teg to spy on us.'

'Yes, he'd be very happy if I wasn't around. He's tried more than once to persuade me, and the rest of the Blessed Council, to go into the Caves of Eternal Rest. If I went, I know the others would follow. He has no right to call himself King. We've only ever had a Queen in Annwn.'

'What happened to the Queen?' asked Jack.

'No one knows for sure, some say she's locked away in one of the rooms of the Citadel, others say she's faded away into nothingness. We wanted her to come to the village but she insisted on staying on the island. I haven't seen her in a very long time. Velindur hasn't allowed her any visitors, that much is true.'

'How did he end up as King then?' asked Camelin.

'You remember that terrible time when all the trouble began?'

'I do,' Camelin replied and touched his head.

Jack could see the line of the scar where Camelin's hair parted. He wasn't likely to forget the Roman hitting him and leaving him for dead. Gwillam looked sad and he seemed lost in thought for a few moments before he continued.

'Velindur did a great service to Annwn. He led the

resistance against the raiders and intruders who came and plundered our land in the past. When the Romans began persecuting the Druids, the four treasures were recalled. The Gateways were to be temporarily sealed until it was safe to reopen them. The Great Sword, the most prized of all the treasures was returned first and the Southern Gateway sealed. The Spear of Justice and the Stone of Destiny arrived, with what was left of the Druids, and the Northern and Eastern Portals were closed. The cauldron you know about.'

'But that doesn't explain how he became King,' said Camelin.

'I'm coming to that. When the Druids escaped into Annwn they were sad and weary. Most of them chose to go into the Caves and spend the rest of eternity in peace. You can't blame them after what they had been through. Velindur saw his chance when only the Blessed Council remained. They were the Lawmakers, the last thirteen Druids in Annwn who worked alongside the Queen. Unlike Velindur, the Council are not strong or ambitious. As each year passed and the Cauldron of Life did not appear, the Queen grew weaker, and her power in Annwn grew less. She was rarely seen, until eventually she wasn't seen at all.'

'Is that when Velindur took over?' asked Jack.

'It is. One day we had a Queen, the next it was a King. No one opposed him because he'd always defended Annwn. At first he spoke for the Queen, and then eventually he began speaking for himself. The Blessed Council still makes the laws, but if he could rid himself of us he'd rule supreme.'

'Why were ravens banished from Annwn?' asked Jack.

'Banished!' exclaimed Camelin.

Gwillam sighed.

'A raven once betrayed the people of Annwn and led a raiding party to the Citadel. They stole the Cauldron of Life. After that it was never kept in one piece and never in Annwn. Some say it was a shape-shifter in the form of a raven, others said it was one of the ravens from the Queen's own garden, which certainly wasn't true, but from that day on, ravens were banished.'

'Here we are,' announced Gavin as he steered the boat into the shallows.

'Thank you,' said Gwillam. 'It's just a short walk from here and then we'll be safe. It would be better not talk until we get back to the village.'

They quickly left the Citadel and Glass Palace behind. Ahead was a crossroads with six paths including the one they'd just walked along. Gwillam pointed to the left.

'The first path leads to the village where the farms and orchards of Annwn can be found. The second takes you straight to the Northern Gate. This middle path leads to the Mother Oak, the next climbs into the mountains and this one leads to my village, where the Druids live. All the members of the Blessed Council live there. Come on, we're nearly there.'

Jack wasn't looking forward to what Nora would say to them. But he didn't have long to wait – she was standing by the first building.

'Thank goodness you're both safe; you've got Charkle and Timmery to thank for your release. If they hadn't found us I don't know what would have happened. Now, let me look at you.'

Nora turned Camelin around and looked him up and down.

'A bit grubby, a few bruises but the rest of you looks like I remember you. Go and bathe first, then get into some proper clothes, after that I've got a job for you. Are you alright Jack?'

'Yes thanks, but I'm a bit hungry.'

'Is that all you ever think about?' grumbled Camelin. 'He's been whingeing about being hungry ever since we got here.'

'That's probably because he hasn't eaten anything. Unlike someone I could mention.'

Jack breathed a sigh of relief. He'd expected Nora to really tell them off. They walked further into the village until they came to the last house. It was bigger than the others and its round thatched roof almost reached the ground. The doorway had strange carvings in the wood. Through it, three steps led down into a large circular room. In the middle was a hearth with a large black pot suspended over the fire. It was cosy inside the house but quite dark after the brightness outside. Gwillam gave Camelin a pile of clothes and steered him back towards the door.

'Down to the waterfall with you, let's get this grime off.'

Camelin pulled a face and looked longingly at the pot of bubbling stew over the hearth.

'Don't worry,' said Nora. 'There'll be plenty left for you.'

Jack hopped up onto a low stool and hung his head so Nora would know he was sorry.

'It's alright Jack, you don't have to explain. We know everything.'

'I am sorry.'

'I know.'

'Where's everyone else?'

'Charkle and Timmery have gone searching. Gwillam doesn't think there are any Dragonettes in Annwn, but I'm sure Charkle will feel a lot better if he's had a look.'

'And Elan?'

'Elan has things to do, she'll be back later.'

'She said I could see her as she really was.'

'And so you shall, but not yet.'

'Gwillam says we're under house arrest, does that mean we have to stay in all the time?'

'Gwillam has a very big house.'

Jack looked at the circular room. It wasn't even as big as Nora's herborium.

Nora laughed.

'This is just the kitchen. There's a doorway over there that leads into another room like this, then another and another. In the middle is a garden so you'll have plenty of room, it's just a shame the trial has to be tomorrow night.'

Jack sighed. He was worried about the trial.

'What happens if they find us guilty?'

'If you've told the truth you'll be fine. When you get to the trial do the same, the truth will set you free. Now how about some food?'

Jack was on his second bowl of stew when Camelin came back. He looked very different. His hair was neat and tidy and he wore a long robe, which was tied with a cord around his waist.

'You could have waited.'

Jack couldn't speak; he had a beak full of food.

'Now, there's the little matter of a punishment for you both,' Nora said once they'd finished eating. 'Follow me.'

She led them through the doorway on the far side of the room. They went through another round room and then out into a large garden. The sunlight was so bright Jack had to put his wing up to shield his eyes from the glare. It took him a few moments to get used to it. Nora stopped before a long wooden table that had been placed in the shade of an old apple tree. On it was the cauldron. The pile of rhubarb stalks lay next to it.

'Oh great,' said Camelin. 'you haven't given it away. I thought you said it was for the King of the Festival?'

'It was, but when we got here and found everything had changed we didn't ask too many questions. We came straight here to find Gwillam. He told us there is no King of the Festival anymore, just a King. We thought we could make better use of it here. There'll be rhubarb pie for supper.'

'Oh rhubarb pie!' said Gwillam. 'What a treat.'

'It will be when Jack's taken out all the strings for me.'

'Strings!' said Jack as he looked closely at the rhubarb. Nora had already taken the leaves off and the tops and bottoms of the stalks had been trimmed, but Jack couldn't see any strings.

Nora picked up the first stick, pinched a piece of the outer skin and pulled. She held up a long fibre for Jack to inspect.

'All these need to be removed or the rhubarb won't be tender. That lot should keep you occupied for a while.'

Camelin started to laugh.

'I'm glad I didn't get that as my punishment.'

'I've got something else for you to do,' said Nora as she pointed towards the cauldron. 'All the little stalks need to be taken off these.'

Jack hopped up to the rim. It was almost full to the top with smooth oval shaped leaves. It would take Camelin an age to destalk them all. Jack noticed Camelin wasn't laughing any more.

'You can enjoy yourselves when you've finished,' Nora told them before going back inside.

When Jack finished destringing the rhubarb he hopped onto the cauldron rim to have a look in. It was still half-full. Camelin sighed. Jack could see his fingers were getting sore. He nudged Camelin on the arm.

'I'll help. You pick up a leaf, I'll nip the stalk off and we'll have them done in no time.'

They worked together in silence and the pile of leaves went down rapidly. Jack got used to the strange taste from the stalks as he nipped them off. Eventually the pile had reduced until there was a great heap of leaves on the table and only a few left at the bottom of the cauldron.

'I'll go and tell Nora we've nearly finished and see what she wants you to do with the leaves.'

'I know what she's going to do with them, she's talked about it often enough over the years. These are the leaves from the Crochan tree. It must have taken them hours to pick this lot. She'll make the elixir tonight.'

'Will she have all her magic back then?'

'She'll have that already. She'll have drunk some of Gwillam's elixir, all Druids know how to make it, it's one of the first things you learn. Nora will brew this up, bottle it and take it back with us through the portal.'

'Does that mean you know how to make it?'

'I know how to prepare it but I wouldn't be able to finish it off, you need magic for that and I didn't used to have a wand.'

'I can't wait till Nora lets us have some wand practice.'

'I've done a bit already, but Nora doesn't know. In fact I might have got a bit of a problem in my loft. I'm going to need your help with it when we get home.'

'We are going to get home, aren't we? They can't keep us here forever, can they?'

Camelin shook his head.

'I don't know what's going to happen. I'm not an expert on the law so it's no use asking me.'

'What kind of a problem in the loft?'

'Well I…'

Camelin stopped abruptly as Nora appeared in the doorway.

'Haven't you two finished yet?'

'Nearly,' said Camelin. 'Jack has and I've only got a few left to do.'

'Hurry up and come inside, we've got visitors, from the Queen.'

'The Queen!' Jack and Camelin said together.

'Yes the Queen. Now come along, everyone's waiting.'

VISITORS

Jack and Camelin followed Nora into the roundhouse. It was full of tall people, all deep in conversation with one other. They were standing around in a circle, but their robes blocked any gaps that Jack might have been able to see through.

'What's going on?' asked Camelin.

'I'm not sure, I'll fly up to that rafter and have a look.'

Below, in the middle of the circle of people was the low table. On top of the table were two pure white birds with bright blue eyes.

'Jack, over here,' piped a familiar voice.

Jack looked around for Timmery but couldn't see him anywhere.

'Over here, we're watching too,' added Charkle.

'Where are you?'

Two tiny, brightly coloured birds appeared and hovered in front of Jack. The smaller of the two was purple with white breast feathers, the other was green with a purple breast.

'Aren't we beautiful? Oh, what an adventure this is turning out to be! We're hummingbirds now,' replied Timmery.

'Hummingbirds!'

'Yes,' said Charkle. 'Timmery couldn't see because of the bright sunshine so Nora turned us both into hummingbirds, there are lots of them here. She said we were a bit conspicuous as bats and we couldn't be Dragonettes because sadly there aren't any here, but it's fun being a hummingbird.'

'So Nora's got all her powers back then?' asked Jack.

'Oh yes, just a flick of her wand and *whoosh*, one minute I'm a bat and can't see a thing, the next I'm a hummingbird. Have you seen my beautiful feathers? I've never had feathers before.'

Timmery darted around Jack's head.

'What's going on?' Camelin called again. 'Who are you talking to?'

'I'll go and tell Camelin if you explain to Jack,' said Charkle. 'It'll save time.'

The purple and green hummingbird flew down and hovered in front of Camelin. Timmery gave a final twirl so that Jack could see all his beautiful purple feathers.

'So why are they all standing around the two white birds?'

'They're ravens, from the Queen's garden.'

'White ravens, it's true then! What are they doing here?'

'They've brought a message for the Blessed Council and for both of you.'

'For us? Why?'

'I don't know. They won't say another word until everyone's here.'

Jack looked around the room. He counted twelve men he didn't recognise. Gwillam was by the doorway and Nora was talking to Gavin.

'So, who's missing?'

'Elan, but she's on her way.'

At last Jack was going to see Elan as she really was.

Gwillam turned to face the crowded room. When a small red hummingbird landed on his shoulder, he banged his staff three times on the floor. The conversation stopped immediately and everyone turned towards the door. The little hummingbird flew into the only space and began to turn around rapidly until all Jack could see was a red blur. Jack watched in amazement as the spinning slowed and Elan appeared.

'That's better,' she said as she shook her shoulders.

'Shall we begin?' Gwillam asked. 'I'm sorry about this being a bit of a squash but Jack and Camelin are under house arrest, which is why we've all had to gather in here.'

The two white ravens cawed loudly and fluffed out their feathers. Once they'd settled Gwillam spoke again.

'Winver and Hesta have brought us all an important message from the Queen of Annwn.'

A low murmur went around the room. When it was quiet Hesta spoke.

'The Queen sends you, her most loyal subjects, a message of hope. By sunset tomorrow there will no longer be a King, his days are at an end. Have faith and soon the rightful sovereign will once more rule in Annwn.'

There was a loud cheer and everyone started talking at once. Gwillam had to bang his staff again.

'Winver has a message too, for Jack and Camelin.'

Jack knew that if he were a boy his cheeks would have been as red as Camelin's. He glided down from the rafter and landed on Camelin's outstretched arm. A pathway opened for them to approach the white ravens. Winver bowed her head slowly before speaking: 'The Queen would like to see you both before the trial begins. You will return to the Citadel with Gwillam and enter the palace by the water gate. When you arrive at the jetty, we will meet you and take you to the palace garden.'

Another murmur went around the room. Jack wondered why they'd been asked to go and see the Queen. No one seemed to know for sure if she was even alive, so why had she sent a message now?

'Will she meet with the Blessed Council before the trial?' one of the men asked.

Hesta shook her head.

'She will speak with the rest of you once the trial has ended and you have arrived at your verdict. She doesn't want to interfere with the Law of Annwn.

Jack's heart sank. He'd hoped she might be going to pardon them. They must be in deeper trouble than he'd imagined. It was the only explanation for why she'd asked to see them.

'Can you stay for a while?' Nora asked the white ravens. 'I'm sure Jack and Camelin have lots of questions to ask you about Annwn.'

'We were told to return to the palace garden once we'd delivered our message. Until tomorrow,' said Hesta as she took off and flew out of the doorway.

'Until tomorrow,' echoed Winver as she followed.

There was silence until Gwillam spoke.

'Shall we continue our meeting at the Mother Oak? She will give us protection from Velindur's spies.'

The assembled Council agreed and one by one filed out of the doorway. Gwillam turned before leaving.

'I'm sorry you can't come with us. We have important things to discuss before tomorrow. You'll see the Mother Oak another time. Maybe Nora will let you help collect the acorns after the trial.'

The room felt empty once the Council had gone. Nora held out her arm for Timmery and Charkle to fly onto and smiled at Jack and Camelin.

'Shall we go into the garden?' suggested Elan. 'We can talk in the sunshine and you can tell me everything that's happened since Nora and I left you outside Glasruhen Gate.'

They all agreed and followed her outside.

'They can't lock us up again, can they?' Jack asked once they'd all finished their account of the day.

Nora didn't answer so Jack looked at Elan.

'If the Blessed Council say you're not guilty, you'll be freed.'

'And if they say we're guilty, what then?' Camelin asked her.

'You'll have a choice. If you insist you're innocent and know you are, you can ask for a second trial, not by men, but by the Spear of Justice. It will not harm anyone who is innocent.'

'What happens if you're guilty and you choose the Spear?' Camelin asked.

'You will die. It's a harsh punishment, which is why very few have ever chosen the Spear. It's instant and final. However, if you prove your innocence and survive, you can demand justice from those who have accused you wrongly.'

'I hope it doesn't come to that,' said Jack. 'I don't think I could stand there while someone threw a spear at me.'

'They don't throw anything,' said Nora. 'Gwillam,

as head of the Blessed Council, has to direct a beam of light from the Spear at the chest of the one accused. Only the Light of Justice can see into someone's heart and know the complete truth.'

Jack shuddered. The joy he'd felt moments before, as they all sat around in the sunshine, had been overshadowed now by a feeling of dread. No one else seemed to notice. Timmery and Charkle were flying around the garden and Nora began to gather up the rhubarb while Elan put the destalked Crochan leaves back into the cauldron.

Jack felt worried. He wasn't looking forward to meeting the Queen of Annwn before the trial. Camelin had been right about the white ravens so he was probably right about the Queen too. He wondered if all her three heads looked the same. Elan smiled at him but he sighed deeply.

'Are you alright Jack?'

'I'm worried about tomorrow.'

'Try not to worry, I'm sure it will all be fine. Is there anything you want to ask me?'

Jack smiled. There was one question he really wanted to know the answer to.

'Will Camelin and I be allowed to collect the acorns from the Mother Oak?'

'Of course you will, but only after the trial. We'll all go together, she's very beautiful, you know. None may approach her without permission, there's a strong magic around her. Only the Druid's are allowed to speak with her. The people of Annwn won't go near her and they don't often come to the Druid's village either.'

'We will get the acorns back in time won't we?'

'You'll see. We'll be home before you know it.'

'Who wants some more rhubarb pie?' Nora asked.

Everyone groaned, said thank you to Nora and left the table. They'd all eaten their fill. Jack looked at Camelin, he'd never known him to refuse any kind of pie before.

'What's wrong? Everyone's gone and Nora won't mind if you have some more, not tonight, I think that's why she left it on the table.'

Camelin sighed and looked wistfully at the pie.

'It's not the same being a boy, I don't feel as hungry.'

'Don't you like being a boy? I thought this was what you wanted?'

'I thought so too, I've longed to come into Annwn for years so I could be a boy again but now it's happened, I'm not so sure. If I stay like this I'll never be able to fly again.'

'But once we go back through Glasruhen Gate you'll be a raven again, won't you?'

'If I go back. Gwillam says I can stay with him and finish my training if I want to. He'll let me be his acolyte again.'

Jack didn't say anything, he had a lump in his throat. They'd only come into Annwn to have a peek at the fair. He hadn't thought that Camelin might want to stay with Gwillam.

'I'd be able to visit you, wouldn't I?'

'Of course you would and I could visit you. Now the portal has been opened it won't ever be closed again, I'm sure of that.'

They were interrupted by a rustling from the branches of the tree they were sitting under. Camelin put his finger up to his lips. Jack hopped onto the lower branch to see if he could see who'd made the noise. He immediately thought of Jed and Teg. Had they somehow managed to get into Gwillam's garden? The sound came again, only closer this time, followed by a high-pitched tittering. Camelin had heard it too.

'Come out,' he called.

Jack expected Charkle and Timmery to burst out of the tree. Instead he saw the two white ravens. Camelin had seen them too. He wondered if the Queen had sent another message. The pair hopped daintily through the branches until they came to rest on either side of Jack.

'We've heard all about you, Jack,' said Hesta, moving closer.

'You're so brave,' added Winver from the other side.

Jack felt very squashed and uncomfortable between the two ravens. He gulped and looked at Camelin for help.

'What you doing here?' asked Camelin.

'We couldn't wait until tomorrow to see you again,' Hesta said to Jack, ignoring Camelin completely.

'Since you couldn't come to see us tonight we thought we'd sneak over here and see you,' Winver explained.

'That's really kind but we have to have an early night, we've got an important day tomorrow,' Jack said hurriedly.

'Isn't he good looking Winver?'

Winver nodded and cocked her head on one side so Jack could see her bright blue eyes.

'I bet you've got lots of girlfriends,' continued Hesta.

Jack spluttered and tried to signal to Camelin to rescue him.

'Oh no, Jack hasn't got any girlfriends, he's too busy being brave,' grumbled Camelin.

Jack suddenly realised Camelin was jealous of all the attention he was getting. This was his chance to turn their attention away from him.

'Camelin's a raven boy you know.'

'A raven boy!' Winver and Hesta said together before collapsing in a fit of giggles.

'He's the best stunt flyer I've ever seen,' continued Jack.

'It's true,' Camelin agreed, 'can either of you fly upside down and do a triple loop-the-loop in the middle of a barrel dive?'

The two white raven's beaks fell open.

'Oooh Camelin! Can you really do that?'

'Oh he can,' said Jack quickly.

Camelin nodded.

'I'm a brilliant stunt flyer.'

Hesta and Winver hopped down to the table. Jack breathed a sigh of relief until they started whispering.

Unfortunately Jack could hear them and by the look on Camelin's face he'd heard them too.

'Which one do you want Hesta?'

'I don't mind, I like them both, which one do you want?'

Jack coughed loudly. Camelin took the hint and held out his arm for Jack to fly onto.

'I'm afraid we're going to have to say goodnight,' said Jack. 'But thank you for coming.'

'Oh you can't go so soon, we've only just got here,' said Hesta.

'We'll see you tomorrow,' added Camelin.

'Please don't tell the Queen we came to see you, she doesn't know. We sort of sneaked out,' pleaded Winver.

'We won't,' Jack assured them.

They were just about to set off for the house when Elan came out. Hesta and Winver both gave a little shriek and quickly took off. Jack let out a sigh of relief.

'What's wrong?' asked Elan.

'Oh nothing, we were just coming in to bed,' replied Camelin.'

'What a coincidence. Nora sent me to fetch you and bring in what might be left of the pie. We've all got a big day tomorrow. Come on, I'll show you to your room.'

They followed Elan through two large circular rooms. The last and largest room had many doors. Elan opened one.

'Try and get some sleep.'

'We will,' replied Jack even though sleep was the last thing on his mind.

Once they were alone, Camelin lay down on the straw pallet whilst Jack perched on the chair.

'So which one do you like best?' laughed Jack.

A pillow hurtled towards him but he ducked before it could hit him.

THE QUEEN'S GARDEN

Jack and Camelin sat down at a long table for breakfast. Gwillam was busy giving orders and making last minute arrangements. Elan was nowhere to be seen. Nora brought them both a bowl of porridge.

'Make sure you use a spoon Camelin. Now you've got hands you're going to have to get used to using them. And no licking the bowl.'

Camelin pulled a face and waggled his head from side to side behind Nora's back, then grudgingly picked up the spoon. Jack chuckled as Camelin grumbled.

'I wish I had my beak back, food just doesn't taste the same without it. It's alright for you; nobody worries about your table manners.'

'That's because Jack's always polite, even when he's a raven,' said Nora as she returned with a pile of clothes before putting them on the end of the table. 'When you've finished breakfast I want you to go and make yourself look presentable. You want to make a good impression, don't you?'

Camelin scowled.

'I'm not going to impress anyone. They've all seen me already.'

'But the Queen hasn't.'

Camelin's mouth fell open.

'You too, Jack, go and sort your feathers out, some of them look a bit crumpled.'

Jack had been so busy worrying about the trial he'd forgotten the Queen had asked to see them. Then he remembered who'd be meeting them. They were going to have to see Winver and Hesta again. He wasn't sure he was looking forward to that.

When everyone was ready they set off for the lake. Gwillam led them in the opposite direction to the way they'd come when they'd arrived. At the end of the village was an open space, in the middle of which stood a large stone.

'This is known as The Clearing, the whole of Annwn can assemble here. The stone in the middle is a monolith, a speaking stone.'

'You mean it talks?' asked Camelin.

'No,' laughed Gwillam. 'Whoever lays their hand upon it has the right to speak, everyone must listen until the speaker has finished. No one may interrupt.'

Camelin stood and looked wistfully at the monolith whilst the others went on ahead.

Jack flew onto his shoulder.

'That monolith's huge! I could do with one of them in my loft for when Timmery calls. I'd keep hold of it all the time, then he wouldn't be able to speak at all.'

'Whilst we're on the subject of the loft, what was that problem you were going to tell me about?'

'I might have tried a little bit of magic out on my own and…'

'What are you two whispering about?' asked Nora.

Camelin's cheeks went red. He was saved from having to answer by Gwillam stopping and pointing towards another signpost.

'The Eastern Crossroads,' he announced.

Again, there were six ways. Gwillam explained where the pathways led.

'The Eastern Gate is straight ahead, the next path climbs up to the mountain, this one goes to the amphitheatre and that one leads to the southern village by the swamp. It's wet and boggy in the lowlands and floods quite regularly. The houses there are built on a platform with a causeway from the village to the dry ground.'

'Amphitheatre?' asked Jack as he looked around.

'You can't see it from here, we're on the wrong side, but those three great hills in the distance are joined together. The middle hillside has seating cut into it all the way up from the ground to the top. It's where the final celebrations take place at the end of every festival when all the people gather together. The best performers entertain the crowd with juggling, storytelling and singing. There's always a mountain of food to share.'

'What kind of food?' asked Jack.

Camelin shook his head.

'Is that all you can think about?'

Jack didn't get a chance to reply as Gwillam sighed and then continued: 'It's all changed now. The people still gather but the treasures aren't brought out. Velindur has them locked away in his room. The Ceremony of the Parting of the Ways hasn't been performed for hundreds of years, not since the last visitors went back through the portals. Nobody's seen the sword, the stone or the spear since then.'

'It's been even longer since the cauldron was here,' added Nora. 'If Velindur knew it was back it would be locked away with the rest of the treasures.'

'Will it be safe in the village? What about Jed and Teg, do they know it's there?' asked Jack.

'It's safe,' replied Nora and smiled. 'A little bit of magic's hidden it away from sight, I doubt anyone's going to bother about a battered old kettle.'

'But what if…' began Camelin.

'If anyone does take a fancy to it they're going to find they've become very attached to it. I've applied a little sticking spell to the handle, they won't be going anywhere if they try to remove it from Gwillam's house.'

They all laughed.

'What happens at the Ceremony, and why is it called the Parting of the Ways?' asked Jack.

Nora sighed and looked longingly at the three hills in the distance.

'It would start after the festivities had ended,

when the light began to fade. It was a beautiful sight. Everyone would light a candle, then the four great treasures would be brought into the arena and their guardians would stand facing in the direction of the gateway to which each one belonged. The guests would rise and make their way to the centre of the arena. They'd stand behind the treasures, and four great processions would make their way to the portals of Annwn. The singing would begin and not stop until the guests were standing in front of their gateway. Anyone who'd accompanied them would say their goodbyes. That was where they would part, until the next visit.'

'Now the cauldron's back, will they do that when we go home?' asked Jack.

'Don't you mean, if we go home? We're still under arrest remember,' grumbled Camelin.

Gwillam put his hand on Camelin's shoulder.

'Try not to worry.'

Nora and Gwillam walked on ahead. Camelin sighed and turned to Jack.

'I only wanted to go to the fair.'

'There'll be another time. We'll be able to go to the fair at Samhain.'

'It's going to be too late at Samhain.'

'Too late for what?'

'To sort out my dustbin.'

'What dustbin?'

'I've been trying to tell you since we got here. You know that bit of magic I tried, well I've got a dustbin in the loft.'

'Why?'

'For emergency supplies of course.'

'How big is it?'

'Dustbin size, like the one we gave Myryl.'

'That big!'

'It seemed a good idea at the time.'

'But what's that got to do with going to the fair in Annwn?'

'I wanted to get an oracular frog. I need to know how many sweets I've got in the dustbin.'

Jack laughed and Nora and Gwillam turned round.

'Shhh! I don't want Nora to know.'

'What are you two laughing about?' asked Nora.

'Camelin was telling me about oracular frogs,' replied Jack.

'I haven't seen one of them in years, they're supposed to be really good at predicting the weather...' began Nora.

'I thought they could predict anything?' interrupted Camelin.

'You won't find many reliable ones, especially not at the fair, they've only got the ones nobody else wants,' said Gwillam.

Camelin made a face and sighed.

Gwillam laughed.

'They're not as good as people make out, you know. Only the males predict the weather.'

'I didn't know that,' replied Camelin and began to drag his heels.

'Never mind,' whispered Jack when Nora and Gwillam had gone on ahead. 'Maybe it wasn't such a good idea to have a dustbin in the loft.'

'What if I don't get to see my loft again? What if they lock me up forever?'

Jack didn't know what to say. What if he wasn't allowed to go home either? He shook his feathers. He wished he were free to fly and explore Annwn. Timmery and Charkle were off now on an adventure. He thought that after the trial he'd ask to go exploring with them. Then he felt guilty – it wouldn't be fair to go without Camelin.

'I wonder where Timmery and Charkle have gone today?'

'Somewhere exciting I expect, where Timmery can practice being brave.'

'Are you grumbling about Timmery again?' asked Nora.

'I just don't think it's fair, they're off having fun, flying around and I've got to walk now. I was remembering what it felt like to fly, to have the breeze ruffling my feathers, to loop-the-loop...'

'Come on,' said Gwillam. 'We'd better hurry or we'll be late, it's this way to the lake. Gavin will be waiting for us with the boat.'

There was a rustling from behind one of the trees. Jack flew up to have a better look. Jed and Teg were crouched behind it. He swooped back down and landed on Gwillam's shoulder.

'We're being followed,' he whispered. 'Do you think they've heard us?'

Gwillam smiled then whispered back.

'That's why I've been giving you the guided tour. We've come to the other side of the lake. There will only be one boat here. They'll either have to swim over to the Citadel or walk all the way round to where the other boats are moored. No one uses this side of the lake anymore and the only way into the Citadel from here is through the water gate, which leads into the Queen's garden.'

'Won't they know where we're going?'

'They might work it out, but by the time they get back to report to Velindur the trial will be well under way. They won't be able to speak to him until after it's over.'

It wasn't long before Jack could see the water's edge. Gavin waved as they approached.

'To the Citadel, boatman,' Gwillam said loudly as he fished into his robe and brought out a large coin. 'Here's your donar.'

Gavin held the boat still while they got in. As soon as they were out of sight of the shore he handed Gwillam the donar back.

'We've only got the one,' he laughed. 'We're hoping that soon we won't be needing donars at all.'

As they got closer to the island Jack could see an archway in a high wall. It was big enough for the boat to go through.

'That's the water gate,' explained Gavin. 'On the other side is a small lake and the Queen's garden is a short walk from there. All the boatmen were forbidden by Velindur to use this entrance, but we've had permission from the Queen herself.'

As the boat drew alongside the jetty two white ravens swooped down from the tree they'd been perched in.

'The Queen sends her greetings to you all,' said Hesta.

'Only Jack and Camelin may enter the garden,' continued Winver. 'She'll see the rest of you later.'

Jack and Camelin got out of the boat and waved goodbye. Jack could hear the two ravens tittering. Hesta hopped forward.

'Do you want to fly on ahead with me, Jack? Winver will bring Camelin.'

'Er… er… I think I'd rather we all stayed together.'

'Thanks,' whispered Camelin.

The two white ravens hopped and skipped ahead towards a beautifully decorated silver gate. As Jack and Camelin approached it swung open. Inside, flowers bloomed everywhere. He could smell honeysuckle. Bees hummed noisily around a plant that cascaded over the tall wall surrounding the garden. In the centre, a black rock stood in a large fountain, water playing over its smooth surface. A group of apple trees provided shade for two stone benches. Hesta and Winver hopped onto one of them.

'Won't you come and sit with us while we wait for the Queen?' croaked Winver.

Jack flew up onto Camelin's shoulder.

'I think I'll stand if you don't mind,' Camelin replied as his looked down at his feet.

A movement from an open door caught their attention. A tall, slender young woman stepped out of the room into the garden. She held out her arms and Hesta and Winver immediately flew onto them and then hopped onto her shoulders. She looked at Jack and Camelin as she spoke: 'You are most welcome. Annwn will be forever grateful to you both for restoring the cauldron and opening Glasruhen Gate. We have waited a long time for this moment.'

Jack felt unsure what to do. This must be the Queen, but she looked serene and very beautiful and didn't have the three heads he'd expected. He swooped to the ground and bowed his head, Camelin bowed too.

'Today will be a turning point in our history. I am restored to my former power thanks to you both. After today, Annwn will once again be the happy place it always used to be, and you two are going to help us to achieve that goal.'

'But how?' asked Camelin then added quickly, 'Your Majesty.'

'By being yourselves and answering any question you may be asked truthfully. Only the truth will set you and the people of Annwn free from Velindur's misguided tyranny. No one, apart from you and my two ravens, know I'm whole again. I doubt any of the people would believe you if you said you'd seen me, but no matter, all will be revealed in time.'

Jack didn't understand what the Queen meant but she spoke so calmly and confidently that he believed every word she said. She reminded him a bit of Arrana in her flowing robe. She was about the same height as Gwillam with a kind face and long chestnut hair. He remembered his Book of Shadows had called her Coragwenelan, Queen of the Fair Folk and Guardian of the Gateways of Annwn. She wasn't wearing a crown or the sort of luxurious cloak Velindur wore. Maybe the robes and crown Velindur had belonged to the Queen. His question was answered when the Queen spoke to Hesta and Winver.

'It's time to get ready for the trial. Bring me my things, then you can escort Jack and Camelin to the Council Chamber.'

Hesta and Winver bobbed twice before swooping through the doorway. They came back carrying a fine white cloak embroidered with silver knot-work designs between them in their beaks. They draped it over the Queen's shoulders and she tied it securely. Next Hesta appeared with a silver girdle. Coragwenelan took it and tied it around her waist. A long black velvet bag hung from one of the branches of the nearest apple tree; she unhooked it and took out a wand, which she tucked into the girdle. Lastly Winver brought a beautiful silver crown encrusted with small pearls. It was interlaced with knots and had an oval moon in the centre. On either side of the moon, facing away from each other were two crescent moons. The Queen slowly put the crown on her head.

'Now we are ready, it's time for you to go. Gwillam will be waiting for you by the Council Chamber. Farewell for now.'

Jack and Camelin bowed low but when they looked up the Queen had gone. Hesta and Winver hopped over to them.

'Come on, follow me Jack,' Hesta coaxed.

Before Camelin could do anything Winver landed on his shoulder and brushed her feathers on his cheek.

'Shall we follow the others?'

203

They made their way through the Palace garden until they came to a high gate. It swung open as they approached and closed behind them. The noise coming from the crowd gathered around one of the glass towers got louder and louder as they approached. Hesta hopped into a sheltered passageway and rapped three times with her beak on a wooden door. Gwillam opened it.

'Thank you,' he said to the white ravens who bobbed up and down. 'I will deliver Jack and Camelin to the chamber. Tell the Queen all is ready.'

'I'm scared,' whispered Jack as he flew up onto Camelin's shoulder.

'So am I,' he replied.

Gwillam smiled encouragingly at them.

'I have to leave you both now. The guards will take you to Velindur.'

A guard, dressed in a yellow and red uniform stepped forward and clamped Camelin's wrists again with the iron cuffs. He tugged hard on the chain to make him walk. Jack heard the door slam and the footsteps of another guard following behind.

TRIAL AND TRIBULATION

It was silent in the Council Chamber except for their footsteps, which echoed around the empty room. Crowds of people had gathered on the other side of the glass walls and Jack felt as if they were in a large goldfish bowl. Camelin and Jack were pushed into the silver cage next to the platform, where Velindur's throne had been placed. The muffled voices from outside grew louder and Jack thought he could hear someone shouting *thief.* Neither of them spoke, but both turned round when a door opened and Velindur strode into the room. His heeled shoes tapped their way across to the cage.

'So we meet again. I hope that whoever is representing you knows they've got a hopeless cause.'

Jack saw Camelin gulp. Neither of them had given a second thought as to who would be defending them at the trial. No one had been to see them or spoken to them. They didn't even know what was going to happen. Velindur must have seen the despair in Camelin's eyes. He started to laugh.

'You haven't got anyone have you? No one's come forward to represent a thief and a shape-shifting spy. No one's willing to make a fool of themselves trying to defend a pair of guilty trespassers. I'm going to enjoy this, what a day I'm going to have. Since I can't lose, I'm going to accuse you both myself. The Blessed Council will have no other choice than to pronounce you guilty when they hear the evidence against you. Then I'll be able to demand justice and choose your fate.'

Jack and Camelin exchanged glances. Velindur walked over to the gathered crowd and raised his arm. The shouts grew louder. As he walked back across the room he muttered to himself: 'It'll only be a matter of time before I can rid myself of those meddlesome Druids for good. I never thought the opening of Glasruhen Gate would bring me such good fortune.'

The door slammed and the noise from outside grew even louder.

'What do we do now?' whispered Jack.

'We're doomed. I'm so sorry I got you into all this. I don't think there's anything Gwillam will be able to do to save us.'

'What about Nora, couldn't she represent us?'

'The guards are still looking for her; she's going to have to stay hidden. She'd be in big trouble if she spoke up for us, he'd probably have her arrested too.'

Camelin sank down to the floor and leant his back against the cage. Jack shuffled over to him and put his head on his knee. Camelin stroked Jack's feathers.

'I am sorry.'

'I know.'

All they could do now was wait until the Blessed Council arrived.

A loud banging on the main door announced the arrival of the thirteen Councillors. Two guards strode over to the door and opened it wide. Once more, the members of the Blessed Council, each dressed in a hooded robe, filed in and made their way to the high-backed chairs around the crescent-shaped table. When they were all in position, the guards closed the doors and marched over to the other side of the room.

'The King,' one announced as the other opened the door.

Velindur walked slowly across the room, his scarlet cloak brushing the floor and his emerald and ruby crown sparkling as he turned his head. He made sure every eye was upon him before he mounted the platform.

'Be seated,' he said to the Councillors and then turned to face Jack and Camelin. 'The prisoners must stand and be brought to the bar.'

Camelin was pulled out of the cage and made to stand in front of a wooden rail, which faced the Blessed Council. Jack was brought out and allowed to perch on it.

'Let the trial commence,' announced Velindur.

The hooded figure at the end of the table stood and addressed the room. Jack recognised Gwillam's voice.

'As the people are a part of this trial, we'd like to open the Chamber.'

Jack could see this idea appealed to Velindur. He was smiled.

'Proceed,' he commanded.

Gwillam pointed his staff at the walls. A bright light hit the glass and there was a gasp from the people as the walls evaporated. The noise was deafening, they all began to speak at once. Velindur held up his hand and the noise stopped.

'Silence for the trial! Who represents the accused?'

No one spoke. Velindur stepped off the platform and paced up and down.

'I ask again, who will represent the prisoners?'

Jack wanted to cry. He could see tears welling up in Camelin's eyes too. Gwillam stepped forward, but before he could speak Velindur interrupted him.

'It is forbidden for a member of the Blessed Council to speak on behalf of a prisoner.'

'I have not come forward to speak on their behalf, no one has come forward. I'd like to appeal to the people.'

Velindur nodded. Gwillam turned and spoke to the crowd.

'Is there anyone willing to speak on behalf of the accused?'

'I will,' replied a tall hooded figure from the back.

Everyone gasped. The crowd parted as the person who'd spoken moved to the front. Jack couldn't see who it was beneath the robes.

'Your name?' Gwillam asked.

'Hynad,' the robed figure replied.

'Nora!' whispered Camelin.

Jack shook his head, he wasn't sure it was Nora. But who else could it be?

Velindur approached the front of the table. He glowered at Hynad before turning and addressing the Council.

'I accuse the boy of being a shape-shifting spy, and the raven a thief. Both have entered Annwn without invitation. It is against the law for any mortal to enter Annwn. I demand punishment, both for the trespass, and the other crimes they've committed.'

The tall hooded woman approached the table and stood next to Velindur. She also addressed the Blessed Council.

'The boy is not a shape-shifter, nor a spy. The raven is not a thief.'

Velindur laughed.

'Is that all you have to say?'

'It is the truth.'

'We will deal with the boy's case first, then the raven. Agreed?'

There was a murmur from the Council and they nodded in approval.

'I call the first witness for the boy's crimes,' announced Velindur.

Jack recognised the guard from the dungeon. He was hustled in front of the table.

'Tell the Blessed Council what happened,' Velindur ordered.

'I took charge of two ravens and locked them in one of the cells. No one came in or went out but when I went back to stop them making a racket one of the ravens was gone and that boy was in its place.'

The crowd murmured. Jack could hear *shape-shifter* being whispered. Velindur smiled to himself then pointed at Camelin.

'Did you shape-shift from a raven to a boy?'

'I'm not a shape-shifter,' Camelin replied in the biggest voice he had so the whole crowd would hear.

Again the crowd muttered. Jack hoped Velindur didn't ask him if he could transform.

'You are a liar,' snapped Velindur. 'I say you shape-shifted.'

Gwillam indicated for Hynad to step forward. She stood before Camelin then turned to face the Blessed Council and the crowd beyond.

'If the boy could shape-shift, why didn't he change back into a raven? Why did he remain a boy?

Why would he want people to know he could change shape?'

Camelin looked hopefully at Jack.

'Who are you?' she asked.

'I'm Camelin, acolyte to Gwillam, High Druid and Keeper of the Shrine in the Sacred Grove by the Holy Oak Well.'

Velindur pointed at Camelin.

'Again I say you lie. We all know Gwillam, he does not have an acolyte and there is no Holy Oak Well in Annwn.'

The crowd agreed. Hynad waited for the noise to subside.

'I call my first witness.'

Velindur looked shocked. Jack wondered who would come forward to speak on Camelin's behalf. The crowd parted again and Gavin made his way to the table.

'Name?' asked Hynad.

'I'm Gavin, former acolyte to Gwillam, leader of the Blessed Council.'

'Gavin,' said Hynad, 'Do you know this boy?'

'I do, his name is Camelin. He became Gwillam's acolyte after me.'

'He lies,' shouted Velindur. 'He's making it up.'

Gavin stood to one side. Velindur looked angry and glowered at Camelin.

'How did you enter into Annwn?'

'I came through Glasruhen Gate.'

'I told you he was a spy. I say you broke into Annwn through the Western Portal.'

'I didn't break in, the gate was open. It was still open when we left it.'

A gasp came from the crowd. Jack could see they were shocked to learn the portal had been opened.

Hynad spoke firmly to the Council.

'If the boy is a spy, why draw attention to himself by leaving the gate open? Wouldn't a spy creep into Annwn unnoticed and close the door behind him?'

Velindur paced up and down.

'I demand to know who sent you, why did you come into Annwn?'

'No one sent me. I came because Glasruhen Gate was open and I wanted to go to the fair.'

Some of the people in the crowd laughed.

'You came as a raven, and you brought a raven with you. Ravens are banned from Annwn. You broke the law,' Velindur shouted.

'I did,' Camelin agreed.

There was silence.

'At last he admits he's guilty. Let the judgement be given.'

Hynad stood before the table.

'I plead the boy be pardoned. He didn't know he was committing a crime, he only wanted to come into Annwn and have some fun at the fair.'

Everything went quiet as each member of the Blessed Council wrote their verdict onto a slate and passed it down to Gwillam. When they were all before him he stood and banged his staff.

'We have agreed on a verdict. We find the prisoner not guilty of shape-shifting or spying.'

The crowd sounded angry and Jack could see Velindur wasn't pleased. Camelin looked relieved. Gwillam banged his staff again for quiet.

'We find the prisoner guilty of trespass.'

'No,' wailed Camelin as he dropped to his knees and tried to fight back the tears.

Velindur strode over to the bar, but before he could speak Hynad touched his arm.

'I beg you, when you decide the boy's fate be just and fair. Don't punish him severely.'

Velindur shrugged her arm off and went over to where Jack was perched and pointed at him. He waited for silence before speaking in his loudest voice.

'The raven is a thief. I call my first witness.'

The woman from the sweet stall at the fair made her way to the table.

'Take a close look at the accused before you speak,' Gwillam told her.

She came up to the bar and peered at Jack.

'That's him! That's the thieving raven who stole my fudge!'

'We saw him too,' a group shouted from the crowd.

'That will be all,' said Velindur. 'I call my second witness.'

The man from the barbecue also went to inspect Jack.

'That's him. He stole a link of my best sausages, seven in all.'

Hynad walked over to the two witnesses.

'How can you be sure this was the same raven who stole your food?'

'He's the raven, no doubt about it,' the woman replied.

'Enough,' cried Velindur. 'He's a thief, he broke the law. Not only did he steal but he ate the food of Annwn without invitation, that also is against the law. Let the Blessed Council make judgement.'

Hynad stepped quickly to the table before the members of the Council could begin to write.

'The raven hasn't had a chance to answer the accusations which have been brought against him.'

Velindur laughed.

'How's a dumb bird going to be able to understand you?'

Gwillam nodded to Hynad to proceed. She walked over to Jack.

'Have you stolen any food since you entered Annwn?'

'No,' Jack croaked as loudly as he could.

Every eye turned towards him. His legs began to tremble. Velindur's mouth fell open; he stared in disbelief as Jack continued speaking.

'I ate nothing that I wasn't offered.'

'You lie. He's a shape-shifting spy too,' cried Velindur.

'Are you a spy?' asked Hynad. 'Can you shape-shift?'

'I'm not a spy and I can't shape-shift. I came into Annwn with my friend Camelin. We wanted to go to the fair.'

'If you're not a shape-shifter, then what are you? Who are you?' Velindur demanded.

'My name is Jack Brenin and I'm a raven-boy.'

The crowd and some of the Blessed Council looked amazed. Velindur began tugging at his cloak as he paced up and down the room.

'That cannot be. I demand a verdict now. You've heard all the evidence.'

There was a lot of muttering and debate amongst the members of the Blessed Council. The slates were passed down to Gwillam. He rose and silence fell.

'We find the prisoner guilty.'

The crowd roared.

Jack's heart sank. He bowed his head.

Hynad stepped forward again.

'I beg you to be lenient.'

Velindur ignored her and marched up to the table.

'Read the prisoners their rights.'

Gwillam stood and unrolled a parchment.

'You have both pleaded not guilty. By the Law of Annwn if you insist you are innocent and the one who has accused you is wrong, you may either accept the punishment the King demands or face the Spear of Justice. If you face the Spear and have told the truth, no harm will come to you. If you lie, you will die.'

A hush fell over the room. Velindur climbed slowly back onto the platform and sat on his throne.

'The law is clear, the penalty is death.'

'No,' wailed Camelin.

Jack froze, he couldn't move, he couldn't speak. He looked at Hynad who stood shaking her head.

'I ask you one last time to reconsider your punishment. The accused came into Annwn believing they would be welcomed not arrested.'

Velindur held up his hand to silence the crowd.

'I have spoken, my word is final.'

Tears ran down Camelin's cheeks. Jack knew he had to be brave. He'd been told to tell the truth and he had. He'd not walked into Annwn he'd flown in, although he didn't think Velindur was in any mood to argue the point. However, he was sure about the other things he'd been accused of. He wasn't totally human anymore, he was a raven-boy. And he certainly hadn't stolen any food.

'I will face the Spear of Justice,' he croaked, but his throat was so dry and his voice so small, only a few people heard.

'No,' Camelin wailed again. 'This is all my fault.'

'What did you say?' Velindur demanded.

Jack summoned all his strength, straightened his back and sat up straight.

'I will face the Spear of Justice. I have told the truth.'

'Fetch the Spear,' Velindur instructed one of the guards.

Jack felt hot tears well up in his eyes. He could hardly bear to look at Gwillam as he walked slowly to the centre of the room and took up his position directly opposite Jack. The room fell silent. No one moved until the door to Velindur's chamber reopened. When the guard stepped out, the crowd started shouting loudly.

'The Spear, the Spear,' they chanted.

The people were making so much noise they didn't hear Gwillam call for silence. He had to bang the Spear on the floor several times, before the noise subsided. When he had silence and every eye was upon him, he held the Spear high for all to see. A murmur from the crowd followed then silence fell again. Jack wanted to close his eyes but he didn't want anyone to know how afraid he felt, instead he swallowed hard and stood very still.

Gwillam grasped the Spear with both hands and bowed his head. He waited for a few seconds, which seemed like hours to Jack. When he looked up again the tip of the Spear was glowing. He held it high again and showed it to the crowd then proclaimed loudly:

'Let the Light of Truth from the Spear of Justice decide the fate of the prisoner.'

'No,' Camelin shouted. 'This is all my fault. Jack didn't eat the sausages, I did.'

No one took any notice. Everyone's eyes were on Gwillam as he aimed the Spear slowly at Jack's heart. When the Spear was horizontal, a shaft of light exploded from the tip, but before it could reach Jack, Camelin launched himself in front of the rapidly moving beam.

'No!' Jack screeched, as Camelin dropped to the floor. 'No!'

He swooped down and tried to choke back his tears as he looked at Camelin's lifeless body.

There was silence. A woman from the crowd cried out and came running over, she dropped to her knees and lifted Camelin's head onto her arm. Jack could see it was Nora even through his tears. She gently put her other arm around Jack's trembling body.

'Arrest her,' Velindur shouted.

Two guards stepped forward.

'Enough!' shouted Hynad. 'I can no longer allow this to continue. The prisoners were telling the truth. They expected to be welcomed here, not imprisoned. They thought they could have fun at the festival and eat their fill as we used to do in happier times. It is true that the Western Gateway has been opened and the Cauldron has been remade. We can thank the raven-boy, Jack Brenin for that.'

Jack heard his name but couldn't speak, there didn't seem to be anything Hynad could do to make anything better, but still she went on speaking. The crowd stood wide-eyed. No one challenged her, no one interrupted.

'The Queen is alive and well.'

'Another lie, Annwn no longer has a Queen. I am your sovereign,' shouted Velindur.

Hynad lowered her hood. Her silver crown glinted in the sunlight. The crowd fell silent. She turned around to face Velindur.

'I tell you again, the Queen is well.'

'Coragwenelan!' he gasped.

'The Queen,' the crowd shouted.

Nora whispered something to Jack but there was so much noise he couldn't hear. He wanted to escape, to fly home, to be anywhere other than here. The Queen continued speaking. She raised her voice above the crowd so they could all hear.

'I pleaded with you to be lenient, to be just and fair. You accused the prisoners unjustly. You were plotting to rid Annwn of the Blessed Council and you must answer for your crime.'

'I wasn't wrong; the boy is dead. You have no proof of the crime you accuse me of.'

Jack knew it was time to speak. He flew back onto the bar, threw back his head and made the call of the raven-owl. The crowd fell silent.

'I heard Velindur planning to be rid of Gwillam. He said if he was out of the way the Blessed Council would do as he wanted.'

'The raven has the right to demand you face the Spear for the injustices you brought upon him. What is it to be Velindur, will you face the Light of Truth or choose banishment from Annwn forever?', asked the Queen.

Velindur lunged at the Queen but Gwillam was quicker and brought his staff between them.

'What will it be, Velindur?'

'I am the King, you cannot just walk in here and take over. If it hadn't been for me Annwn would have been ransacked. I closed the portals and kept our land safe. You should be bowing down to me instead of threatening me with punishment.'

'Let the people decide,' said the Queen. 'I offer you peace and prosperity. Now I am whole again, we can once more open the portals. We can again be the happy realm we used to be. The Earth has changed, we are no longer under threat. Humankind has no interest in us anymore.'

'The Earth has not changed. People are selfish, there has never been anyone born on Earth who has done a selfless act.'

'I dispute that,' said Nora.

'Do you know of a selfless mortal?'

'I do, he stands before you now.'

The people looked around to see who Nora meant.

'Jack Brenin was granted the power of Annwn by Arrana.'

Cries of amazement came from the crowd.

'For his courage, bravery and selflessness in helping us to restore the Cauldron of Life, Arrana granted him a wish.'

Velindur laughed.

'He probably helped you so he could come and plunder Annwn once you'd opened Glasruhen Gate. What could he possibly have asked for that wasn't selfish.'

'He asked for a lath for Camelin.'

The crowd murmured and fell silent as Nora continued.

'A totally selfless act.'

'Why didn't he ask for a lath for himself?'

'He didn't need to. He'd already been granted one by Arrana.'

'You have no proof this.'

'Oh but we have,' said Nora as she produced Jack's wand. She held it high for all to see then placed it in Jack's beak. It immediately became smooth.

The Queen turned again to the crowd.

'It is your decision: King or Queen?'

'Queen, Queen, Queen,' the crowd chanted.

Coragwenelan bowed to the crowd and then turned to Velindur.

'The Spear of Justice or banishment?'

'You won't get rid of me that easily. You're all going to be sorry for treating me like this. One day I'll have my revenge, you'll see.'

'I presume you choose to be banished then?'

'You leave me with little choice. I will not face the Spear.'

Coragwenelan produced her own wand and Gwillam took a small jar from his pocket.

'*Vespula*,' the Queen cried as she aimed her wand at Velindur.

He wobbled from side to side as he began to shrink. Gwillam took the lid off the jar and waited until the transformation was complete and a small wasp emerged from the scarlet cloak which lay on the floor. He captured the angry creature, closed the lid and passed the jar to one of the Blessed Council to look after.

'We'll deal with him later. For now we have more important things to attend to,' said Gwillam as he made his way over to Camelin.

'Everything's going to be alright now,' Nora told Jack.

Jack didn't see how anything could ever be right again. Camelin had sacrificed himself; he'd lost his best friend. He suddenly felt exhausted. He hopped down to the floor.

'What happened?' groaned Camelin.

'You're alive!' cried Jack. 'But how?'

Tears of joy replaced Jack's tears of sorrow. Camelin sat up slowly and shook his head. He felt his chest then checked his arms and legs.

'I feel really dizzy.'

'You'll be fine,' Nora assured him. 'You've had quite a jolt but in a couple of hours you'll be your usual self again.'

Jack was speechless. He was overjoyed that Camelin wasn't hurt. Nora stood and began to explain.

'I'm sorry Jack. When I came over I tried to tell you he was only stunned, but you couldn't hear me.

Then everything happened so fast. Camelin only spoke the truth. He even admitted he'd eaten the sausages. The Spear of Justice could not harm him.'

'I told the truth too. I'd have been alright, wouldn't I?'

'I couldn't let you take that chance,' Camelin replied. 'It was my fault we got into trouble.'

'We'll talk about this later,' said Nora. 'Now I think it's time we all went back to Gwillam's house for a rest before the Festival tonight. It's been quite a day.'

'Festival?' said Camelin. 'As in we can go round the fair and have some fun?'

'When I'm sure you're both alright,' agreed Nora.

'I feel better already,' said Camelin.

'Me too,' agreed Jack.

'I'd like you all to come to my garden before you go back to the village,' said Coragwenelan. 'I have something very special to show you. Timmery, Charkle and Elan will be there too.'

'To the garden then,' said Gwillam.

They all followed the Queen out of the Council Chamber.

LITTLE ACORNS

Jack's heart was still beating wildly as they made
their way back to the Queen's garden. The strain of the
last few hours had drained him of energy. He hadn't
had the jolt Camelin had received from the Spear but
he still felt dizzy. He was also hungry; it was well past
lunchtime. The smell of food wafting on the breeze and
his growling stomach confirmed that he needed to eat.

'Was that you?' asked Camelin.

'Sorry,' Jack replied. 'I could eat a mountain, I'm
that hungry.'

'Don't worry I'll get you some food.'

Jack wondered if Camelin was going to do his
shuffle dance to impress everyone, but he somehow

didn't think it would be as good, now he was a boy. Camelin stopped, put his hand to his head and wailed.

'Oooh! I feel so dizzy, I think I need food.'

Nora fussed around and supported him under his arm.

'It won't be long. I'm sure we can ask for something from the Queen's kitchen. Do you think you can make it that far?'

'I think so,' Camelin replied in his wobbliest voice.

They'd dropped behind the rest, but Nora didn't hurry to catch up.

'Are you two alright now?'

'Yes,' Jack replied and gave Camelin a look so he wouldn't overact too much.

'We had no idea how the trial was going to go. All we'd had was a message from the Queen. Only Gwillam and I knew she was going to represent you. We just put our trust in you to tell the truth, and you did. You were so brave inside the Council Chamber.'

'So brave,' echoed two voices from above.

Jack looked up. Hesta and Winver were perched on the wall. They giggled when Camelin went red.

'The Queen sent us to tell you dinner's ready,' said Hesta.

'I'm sorry,' said Nora. 'Camelin's still not feeling very well. We'll get there as soon as we can.'

'We'd better hurry,' said Jack. 'We don't want it all to be gone by the time we get there.'

'Oh it won't be gone,' replied Winver. 'You two are the guests of honour and they won't start without you.'

The garden looked slightly different. A long trestle table, laden with all kinds of food, stood under the shade of the apple trees now.

'Oh wow! Look at all that food!' exclaimed Jack. 'Aren't you excited Camelin?'

'I would be if I was a raven again, I'd really enjoy that lot. Now, I'm hungry, but not like I used to be. Food just doesn't taste as good anymore. And I don't like not being able to fly. Now we're free we can explore but it won't be the same if I have to walk.'

Gwillam overheard and, looking sad said: 'I thought you'd decided to be my acolyte again and finish your training.'

Camelin replied: 'I don't feel right as a boy, it's not much fun. I think I'd rather go home with Nora and Jack than stay here, if you don't mind. We'd be able to come back and visit you, wouldn't we?'

'Of course you can visit, and Jack too. Maybe Nora can finish off your training. You'll need to be able to read and write now you've got your own wand.'

'But I can read and write.'

Gwillam looked at Nora.

'It wasn't me, I didn't teach him; Jack did.'

'Look,' said Camelin as he picked up a stick and scratched his name in the earth.

Jack could see Gwillam was impressed. Camelin didn't say he'd only just learnt and needed a lot more practice.

'Nora's given me a Book of Shadows, you'll be able to write to me,' said Gwillam.

Jack smiled. Gwillam would find out for himself just how bad Camelin's spelling was.

'Maybe you could write to us too,' said Winver as she flashed her bright blue eyes at Camelin. 'We know how to write.'

Camelin swallowed hard but didn't answer.

'I can't wait to see you as a raven,' continued Winver. 'I bet you're very handsome, don't you Hesta?'

'Not as handsome as Jack.'

Now it was Jack's turn to feel embarrassed. He was relieved when Elan appeared in the doorway with Timmery and Charkle hovering above her head.

'Oh Jack,' cried Timmery. 'We've heard all about the trial. You were both so brave.'

'Yes, we were,' agreed Camelin.

'Are you alright?' asked Elan.

'We are,' replied Jack.

Everyone waited expectantly for the Queen to appear. A noise from inside the room made them turn around. An old woman, about Nora's age appeared, followed by a younger one.

'Can I present to you my mother, Cora, and my grandmother Gwen,' said Elan.

Gwillam bowed.

'Your Majesty,' he said, 'I think it's time to reveal your secret to your most loyal subjects.'

Elan, Gwen and Cora bowed their heads together. They joined hands and held them high in the air. A breeze wafted around them, which slowly increased until a small whirlwind engulfed them and they began to spin. The brightest colours Jack had ever seen sparked in all directions. When the spinning stopped the Queen stepped out of the bright light. Jack and Camelin looked astonished.

'But...' gulped Camelin.

'You're the Queen, all three of you, Cora, Gwen and Elan,' exclaimed Jack. 'You said I could see you as you really were in Annwn. And to think, I thought you were a hummingbird!'

'No one except Nora and Gwillam have ever known,' explained Coragwenelan. 'When Elan got trapped on Earth we were no longer able to appear as the Queen. We needed to be together to transform. We didn't realise until it was too late and by then we'd lost most of our power. If you hadn't opened Glasruhen Gate, Annwn would never again have had a Queen; it would have been left to the mercy of Velindur.'

'There's not much mercy in that man,' interrupted Camelin then went red when he remembered who he was talking to and added: 'Your Majesty.'

They all laughed.

'If you don't mind we're going to separate, we feel better as three people. It's been so long since we've been Coragwenelan that it still feels strange being together.'

'I know what you mean,' grumbled Camelin. 'I wish I could turn back into a raven. I'm not sure I like being a boy.'

'Do you truly wish to be a raven again?' Coragwenelan asked. 'We can grant your wish. You have done so much for Annwn it's the least we can do for you.'

232

'Oh please! Make me a raven again.'

Coragwenelan took her wand from her silver girdle and twirled it around. She sent colours spinning around Camelin's body until he was lost from sight. As the colours subsided a dark shape could be seen.

'You did it,' he croaked and hopped around. 'You did it, I'm myself again. When can we eat? I'm starving!'

Jack saw Winver nudge Hesta. Camelin was too busy eyeing up the food to notice.

'See, I said he'd be handsome.'

Coragwenelan raised both hands in the air and began to spin around again. Through the explosion of coloured light Jack could see three separate figures forming until Cora, Gwen and Elan stood before them. Jack's stomach growled and Camelin's replied.

'I think we ought to eat before Camelin collapses again,' laughed Elan.

'Camelin's had his wish, what would you like Jack?' asked Elan when they'd all finished eating. 'It should be something you'd like for yourself, you deserve it.'

Jack didn't have to think, he knew exactly what he wanted.

'I'd like to see the Mother Oak when you go to collect the acorns.'

'We can grant that easily. We'll meet you back at Gwillam's house later and then go to the Mother Oak together.'

'Thank you.'

'Now Camelin can fly again, why don't you go and explore Annwn?' said Nora.

'Great,' said Camelin through a beak full of food. 'D'you know this is the best apple pie I've ever tasted.'

'That's a compliment, he's tasted quite a few,' laughed Elan.

'Can we come too?' asked Hesta.

'Sorry, boys only,' replied Camelin.

'Ooh, wonderful, that means we can go Charkle,' said Timmery.

Camelin scowled.

'Of course you can come,' Jack told the two hummingbirds. 'We'd be pleased to have you on our *boy's* outing.'

Hesta and Winver looked disappointed.

'We'll see you at the Festival celebrations later

on then. Maybe we could go round the fair together?' suggested Winver.

Nora smiled.

'That would be lovely, wouldn't it boys?'

They nodded, but without any enthusiasm.

'Come on, what are we waiting for?' said Camelin. 'We've got things to do, places to go, and lots to see. Ready?'

As they flew out of the garden Jack's heart felt ready to explode. He was so happy. They were free and off exploring together.

'Where to first?' Jack shouted.

'How about the mountains? They're amazing, you can see right through into the Caves of Eternal Rest where the Druids are sleeping,' said Timmery.

'To the mountains,' Camelin croaked as he did a triple loop-the-loop before going into a barrel roll.

'Now you?'

'I'm not ready to do that yet,' replied Jack.

Charkle flew rapidly towards Camelin then at the last minute he reversed his wings and flew backwards.

'Show off,' grumbled Camelin as they flew off in the direction of the mountains.

As the mountains loomed above them the air temperature dropped. They'd left the fields and the forest and the warmth of the sun behind. Now, in the shade of the tall snow-capped peaks, it felt very cool.

'Over here,' shouted Charkle. 'The entrance is this way.'

As Jack swooped down towards the cliff face he could see a ledge. A path wound around the mountain to a natural arch in the rock. Something that looked like a piece of glass covered the mouth of the cave. Timmery hovered in front of it.

'Come and look, you can see right through it.'

Jack peered in. What he thought was glass turned out to be a sheet of ice.

'Oh Camelin, look at this,' he cried.

Camelin flew over and landed on the ledge. He cocked his head and peered in.

'Wow! Are they jewels?'

'No, they're crystals,' replied Charkle. 'We found out a lot about this cave. No one can break in. The ice is magic, the Druids put it there when they sealed themselves in. They decided on this cave because it's full of natural crystals which give out their own light.'

'Everyone knows where the cave is, but because it's sealed from the inside no one can get in,' added

Timmery. 'See that enormous diamond? If it's turned three times, the ice will melt and then they could come out.'

Jack looked at the diamond. It gleamed even though there wasn't any sunlight. The whole cave sparkled.

'Do you think they'll want to come out now Velindur's gone?' asked Jack.

'How're they going to know what's happened if they're asleep?' replied Camelin.

'Maybe Gwillam knows how to wake them up,' suggested Timmery. 'I'm sure they'd want to know the Queen's returned.'

They stayed for a while longer and marvelled at the cave. For as far as they could see, stone niches had been cut into the walls. Inside each one lay a Druid with a wand by his side and a staff across his sleeping body.

'I'm getting cold,' said Charkle.

'Me too,' agreed Camelin.

'Time to go,' announced Timmery. 'Back to the village, follow me.'

'There you are,' said Nora as they flew into Gwillam's house.

They all started talking at once as they tried to tell Nora about the amazing things they'd seen, until she put her hand up for them to stop.

'I thought you wanted to go to the Mother Oak. If you carry on like this we'll not get there and back before the fair ends, you did say you wanted to go round the stalls before the Festival, didn't you?'

They all agreed.

'We're ready. We've just been waiting for you to arrive.'

Jack looked round to see Gwillam and Elan standing in the doorway. Elan was holding a leather pouch.

'For the acorns,' she explained.

'How many do we need?' asked Jack.

'As many as the Mother Oak decides we can have,' said Nora. 'We need to explain the situation and she will give us what we require to put things right on Earth.'

'Shall we go?' asked Gwillam.

Nora turned to Timmery and Charkle.

'Would you two mind staying here? We have the little matter of a rather angry wasp who might need guarding. We wouldn't want the jar to get into the wrong hands.'

The two little birds hovered in front of the jar Gwillam had placed on the table.

'It will be our honour to guard the house while you're gone,' replied Timmery. 'We'll make sure no one touches the jar.'

'They'll get a warm welcome if they try,' laughed Charkle as he blew a column of fire towards the hearth.

Jack and Camelin raced and chased, swooped and dived, as they made their way northwards.

'Look!' croaked Camelin. 'We're nearly there.'

'She's enormous,' said Jack. 'Even bigger than Arrana. What are all those bushy bits growing in her branches?'

'Mistletoe!' croaked Camelin. 'Thank goodness Hesta and Winver aren't here, we wouldn't have stood a chance. Girls can kiss you if you stand under the tiniest bit of mistletoe.'

'Don't you go sitting in her branches,' called Nora as Camelin swooped past her. 'Wait patiently we'll be there in a minute.'

Jack and Camelin landed in front of the great oak. Her trunk was nearly as wide as Gwillam's house and her branches spread almost to the floor. Jack's neck ached as he craned to see the top. Unlike Arrana, the Mother Oak stood alone. A carpet of blue and white flowers surrounded her but no other tree was within sight.

'She's more beautiful than I remembered,' whispered Nora.

As Elan and Gwillam joined them, there was a rustling from behind the Mother Oak and two Dryads peeked out from behind the trunk. As they came forward, their long silver hair flowed in the breeze and their silken gossamer dresses shimmered in the afternoon sun.

'Fernella and Fernilla!' cried Elan. 'It's been so long since I've seen you.'

The two Dryads curtsied.

'We have waited patiently for your return, we always knew one day you would come. We heard the Cauldron had been remade,' said Fernella.

'Our Mother Oak is ready to entrust her children to you,' added Fernilla.

Jack hadn't realised the Mother Oak would think of her acorns as children, it would mean Arrana was her child too. Nora stepped closer and Gwillam raised his staff. He banged it three times on the earth before Nora spoke.

'Sylvana, Mother of all Hamadryads, Guardian of the Oaks and Bearer of the Sacred Mistletoe, we have a request to make of you.'

There was a rustling and shaking of branches, the trunk began to ripple and sway until it disappeared and a beautiful old woman stood towering above them. Her silver hair cascaded down to her ankles. She smiled.

'Eleanor, Seanchai, Keeper of Secrets and Ancient Rituals, Guardian of the Sacred Grove, you have returned. You have opened Glasruhen Gate at last. How are my daughters?'

'The news isn't good Sylvana. We spent many years searching for the cauldron plates in vain. We were only able to find *that which was lost* when Jack Brenin, agreed to help us.'

Jack bowed low at the mention of his name.

Camelin coughed.

'He was greatly helped by Camelin, acolyte to Gwillam, High Druid and now Leader of the Blessed Council in Annwn.'

Camelin hopped over to Jack and bowed too.

'How many of my daughters are left?' Sylvana asked Nora.

'Only Arrana. And she is fading fast.'

Sylvana closed her eyes and held her breath before letting out a great sigh.

'This is not the news I had hoped to hear. You must take enough acorns to repopulate the forests with Hamadryads once more. It makes my heart glad to know that with your help my daughters will once again live on Earth.'

Nora bowed before answering Sylvana.

'Once Arrana has transferred her knowledge into the acorns, all the forests will once more have the protection they need. There need never be hollow trees on Earth again.'

Sylvana looked at each of them in turn.

'Is that Elan I see with you?'

Elan stepped closer.

'This is a happy day for Annwn. The Queen has returned, now Annwn will be restored to the peaceful and happy land it used to be. You will all come and visit us often, won't you?'

They all agreed. This was one of the happiest days of Jack's life too.

'Now, Eleanor, if you will step forward I will give you my acorns. Take good care of them, tend them well and be a friend to them all.'

Sylvana cupped her hands and blew gently over her palms, when she lowered her hands towards Nora they were full of large acorns. They were the same shape and size as Nora's golden acorn, but instead of being gold they were a deep forest green.

'Thank you,' said Nora as she took each one from Sylvana's cupped hands and placed it carefully into the leather pouch Elan held open. 'It has been a long journey for us all, but now we truly can restore what was lost. The forests will live again.'

'Will you come again soon, Gwillam?' Sylvana asked.

'I will,' he promised. 'Nora has brought me a Book of Shadows so she'll be able to write to me and I can tell you the news from Earth.'

'I shall look forward to that. Fernella and Fernilla keep me well informed about Annwn, but news from my children on Earth will be most welcome.'

Sylvana seemed satisfied that her task was complete. She smiled and once more began to shimmer and shake. It wasn't long before she'd completely disappeared and only the gnarled trunk stood before them. The two Dryads curtsied then hurried behind Sylvana's trunk. Nora sighed and Gwillam patted her on the shoulder.

'We'd better see about getting you all ready for home.'

'But you said we could go round the fair and see the Festival,' complained Camelin.

'And so you shall. Your journey home begins after the Festival ends. Shall we make our way to the fair?'

'Oh yes please!' said Jack and Camelin together.

THE PARTING OF THE WAYS

As they drew near the fair the noise grew louder. Jack was worried in case people were going to shout at them again. Instead, the moment the men on stilts saw them they pointed and the crowd cheered as they flew overhead.

'Now that's a better welcome,' said Camelin.

'Where do you want to go first?' asked Jack.

'The storyteller,' replied two piping voices from behind.

'I thought you were guarding a jar for Gwillam and Nora,' grumbled Camelin.

'We were,' said Charkle. 'But they said we should come over to the fair and have some fun too.'

'You seem to have had lots of fun already,' grumbled Camelin.

'Oh we have, we have,' agreed Timmery.

'Well we're going this way and the storytelling looks like it's over there.'

Timmery and Charkle flitted off towards a group of people crowded around a tall, cloaked figure holding a story staff.

'Come on Jack, follow me. You've got to taste those sausages.'

'But we still don't have any money.'

'Let's try the shuffle dance, we can both do it. We'll ask to be paid in sausages.'

'OK, I suppose we could try.'

They flew over to the barbecue and landed on a branch overhanging the grill.

'Just smell that,' said Camelin as he breathed deeply.

'They do smell good,' agreed Jack.

'It's performance time, ready?'

'Ready.'

Camelin led and Jack followed. They shuffled up and down the branch rocking from side to side then bobbing up and down. A crowd began to gather but instead of shouting they cheered and clapped. Camelin did a one-footed twirl then nodded his head to an invisible beat whilst shuffling sideways.

'Come on down,' the man behind the barbecue called. 'I presume you'd like some sausages?'

'Oh yes please!' replied Jack. 'But we still don't have any money.'

'They're free to you two. From what I hear you deserve a lot more, it's the least I can do, now I know who you are.'

The crowd cheered again. Jack could hear other stallholders shouting for them to come and sample their food, when they'd finished at the barbecue. Camelin looked extremely happy.

'Now, aren't they the most delicious sausages you've ever tasted?'

'They are, but I'm going to leave room for some of the other things. Didn't you say the pies were good too?'

Jack was relieved when they finally went to join Timmery and Charkle on a branch overlooking the storyteller.

'You missed the *Glasruhen Giant*,' twittered Timmery. 'It wasn't the same as the one Nora tells, but it was still good.'

'*The Dragon of Howling Hill* was brilliant,' added Charkle. 'You're just in time, you haven't missed them all. The storyteller's got one more left.'

Jack tried to get into a comfortable position so he could enjoy the next story. He groaned.

'My stomach feels fit to burst.'

'Yeh, so does mine, great isn't it?'

Jack wasn't sure he liked feeling so full, but he had to agree with Camelin that he'd just eaten some of the most delicious food he'd ever tasted.

The storyteller banged his staff three times and the gathered crowd fell silent.

'My tale comes from a time long ago, in a land far away beyond the four portals of our world...'

Jack was worried he might fall asleep, the storyteller's voice was so soft and quiet, but it turned out to be a really good story called *The Rat and the Treacle Vat*. He listened carefully so he'd be able to retell it to Motley, Orin and the Night Guard when they got home. At the end of the tale the crowd cheered loudly.

'Can we go and see the jugglers now?' asked Jack. 'I love watching them; I wish I could do it.'

'Not much chance as a raven,' replied Camelin. 'But there's no reason why you can't teach yourself when we get back.'

'I might just do that.'

'Jugglers are this way,' piped Timmery. 'Follow me.'

Camelin sighed.

'He likes to be in charge, doesn't he?'

They all followed Timmery to another group, where the men on stilts were throwing batons to each other. Jack counted five in the air at once.

'Grandstand view,' called Camelin as he swooped onto a branch close by.

They all followed.

'We're going to look at the stalls now,' Camelin announced when the juggling had finished. 'Just me and Jack, we'll see you at the fun fair later.'

Timmery looked disappointed but Charkle didn't seem to mind.

'Couldn't they have come too?' asked Jack as they flew towards to the circle of oaks.

'No, I want to show you something and I need you to help me choose which one to get.'

'Choose what?'

Camelin didn't answer, he was too far ahead. Jack followed and swooped down when Camelin landed behind the only tree without a table.

'What's wrong?' asked Jack.

'Nothing, we're waiting.'

'Waiting for what?'

'For Gavin.'

Jack was about to ask why, when Gavin appeared.

'Ready you two?'

'Ready,' said Camelin.

'Ready for what?' asked Jack.

'I've got a plan and Gavin's agreed to help. Come on, they're over here.'

Camelin hopped and skipped over to one of the stalls next to a small pond. Jack and Gavin followed. Camelin peered into the water.

'What are you looking for?' asked Jack.

Before Camelin could answer the stallholder bustled over and spoke to Gavin:

'Now, what kind of oracular frog would you be wanting sir? We've got frogs what forecast rain or snow, showers or storms. You name it and we'll find you the right one.'

'I'd like to choose my own if you don't mind' said Gavin. 'I'll have a look and see what you've got before I decide.'

The stallholder banged a small gong that hung over the pond. Several green heads appeared, followed by loud croaking.

'Look lively, boys! Who's going to be the lucky chap who goes to a new home today?'

The croaking increased as the frogs hopped onto three large lily pads. When the stallholder moved away, Camelin shuffled up to the edge of the pond.

'What d'you think Jack?'

'About what?'

'Which one to choose. I don't know which one's going to be best.'

Gavin laughed.

'Are you sure this will work?'

'Of course it will. Gwillam said he didn't have any use for the money anymore and you did say you'd buy me anything I wanted from the fair. You buy the oracular frog with the donar and then give it to me as a present to take home. What's wrong with that? I just don't know which one to choose.'

'Try them out,' suggested Jack. 'Ask them a question.'

Gavin looked at the frogs and they all looked expectantly back at him.

'When will it snow in Annwn?' he asked.

'Never,' chorused all the frogs except one.

'I'll have that one,' said Camelin and nodded at the only frog that hadn't spoken.

'You don't want that one,' said Gavin. 'It's no good if it can't predict the weather.'

'I know what I'm doing, that's the one I want.'

Gavin went over to the stallholder and pointed to the frog: 'I'll take this one please.'

'Your choice,' laughed the man as he netted the frog and dropped it into a jar. He tied a string around the neck and passed it to Gwillam, in exchange for the donar.

Camelin looked pleased.

'You won't forget to bring it to the Festival later will you? Nora won't be able to say I can't have it if you give it to me as a present.'

'I won't forget,' laughed Gavin as he waved goodbye.

Camelin did a little twirl.

'I've got an oracular frog,' he chanted as he jigged around.

Jack didn't understand.

'But it was the only one that didn't speak. What if it never speaks. What if it isn't an oracular frog at all?'

'I don't need one to predict the weather.'

'What do you want it for?'

'To predict how many sweets are in my dustbin. That's the sort of important thing anyone would want to know.'

Jack laughed. He couldn't wait to get back to Camelin's loft and see the dustbin. He hoped the little frog was going to live up to Camelin's expectations.

The fun fair was crowded. Jack was grateful he could fly and didn't have to try to battle his way through the crowds. They stopped to watch people trying to throw horseshoes onto a peg in the ground. There was a wooden bowling alley with skittles. A couple of men were arm wrestling.

'You need hands to have a go at any of this lot. Isn't there anything you can do if you've got wings?' grumbled Camelin.

'Jack, Camelin, over here,' chirruped Timmery and Charkle.

The two little hummingbirds led the way as they darted above the crowd until they reached a tall building. It looked like a gigantic upside-down ice-cream cone.

'It's a helter-skelter,' cried Jack. 'They're great fun.'

Timmery flitted around Camelin's head.

'Can I sit on your head when you go down?'

'No you can't,' grumbled Camelin.

'It's alright. You can sit on mine,'

'Thank you, thank you,' said Timmery. 'Come on, let's have a go.'

Camelin tutted before flying to the top of the ride. Jack decided to let him have his own mat.

'Hold tight,' Jack croaked.

'Wheeeeeee!' cried Charkle and Timmery as they whizzed around the helter-skelter.

'That was brilliant,' said Jack. 'Shall we do it again?'

They'd just set off on their second run, when Hesta and Winver arrived. They flew around the outside of the helter-skelter and followed Jack as he made his way to the bottom.

'We've been looking everywhere for you,' said Hesta before giggling loudly.

Jack could hear Camelin groan.

'We're busy,' he said. 'Too busy to talk.'

'We've not come to talk.'

Jack gulped and looked around quickly in case there was any mistletoe about.

'The Queen's asked us to come and find you,' continued Winver. 'You have to go back to Gwillam's house. It's almost time for the Festival and you two are to be the guests of honour.'

Hesta laughed.

'There are going to be two perches for us to share at the amphitheatre, right next to the Queen's throne.'

Jack and Camelin didn't say anything.

'Isn't that wonderful?' said Timmery.

'They're not for you,' replied Camelin.

'We're all going to sit next to the Queen, Timmery and Charkle too.'

Camelin humphed and, without another word to anyone, took off in the direction of Gwillam's house. Jack, Timmery and Charkle gave Hesta and Winver an embarrassed smile then flew after him.

Gwillam was waiting for them by the door.

'I'm glad you came straight away, you're to be…'

'The guests of honour,' Camelin said.

'How did you know?'

'Hesta and Winver told us.'

'No matter, we need to get everything together. You'll be going straight on to Glasruhen Gate when the Festival ends.'

Jack's heart missed a beat. He'd been having so much fun he'd almost forgotten why Elan and Nora had come into Annwn in the first place. Now they were going home, tonight.

'The Queen will be waiting for us, are you ready?' asked Nora.

They all nodded. Gwillam and Gavin picked up the cauldron between them. Jack could see his and Camelin's wands inside it along with the acorn-filled leather bag. Nora stepped out of the house then dashed back inside. She came out with the jar, which still had an angry-looking wasp buzzing around inside it.

'We nearly forgot this!'

Jack looked at the jar. He had the uncomfortable feeling that the wasp was staring at him.

'What will happen to Velindur? Will he be a wasp forever?'

'Oh no,' replied Gwillam. 'Once he's been released the transformation spell will wear off. But he'll never be able to enter Annwn again. If he does he'll turn back into a wasp and have to stay like that forever.'

An even angrier wasp buzzed in the jar. Nora put it inside the cauldron with the rest of the things they were taking back through the portal.

'Will the other three gateways be opened again now the Queen is back?' asked Camelin.

'That will be for the Blessed Council to decide, but I know the Queen would like to reopen them,' answered Nora.

Jack couldn't get used to Elan being a part of the Queen. It felt strange without her.

'Come on,' said Nora. 'We need to go or we're going to be late and you two are going to be...'

'The guests of honour,' said Camelin. 'We know, we've been told.'

They made their way from the village past the clearing where the Monolith stood. As they entered the amphitheatre the crowd stood and cheered. The Queen sat on a beautiful throne that was covered in silver runes. She clapped too as they made their way towards her. Camelin and Charkle were shown to a perch to the left of the Queen, and Jack and Timmery were offered the one on the right. Hesta landed next to Jack. He looked over at Camelin, Winver was already next to him. The Queen held up her hand to the crowd and they fell silent.

'Let the festivities begin,' she cried.

The best jugglers, storytellers and singers entertained the crowd until the light began to fade. When the sky darkened Nora took a candle to Coragwenelan then passed one to each of the others. Everyone in the crowd got their candles out too.

'Please allow me,' said Charkle and he blew a small flame towards the Queen's candle. Nora lit hers from the Queen's and one by one the flame was passed from one candle to the next until the whole amphitheatre was filled with flickering light.

'Bring forth the Treasures,' Gwillam cried, banging his staff on the ground three times.

Three hooded figures advanced to the centre of the amphitheatre, each bearing one of the Treasures of Annwn. Nora pulled up her hood, picked up the cauldron and joined the others in the middle of the arena and then turned to face the Western Gate. It was the first time Jack had seen the Sword of Power. It was very big. The hooded figure held it high above his head and faced the Southern Gate. Another tall figure held the Spear of Justice by his side and faced towards the North Gate. Jack was amazed when he saw the Stone of Destiny, he hadn't realised it would be so beautiful. It too was held high and the light from the candles flickered on its green and blue surface as it was pointed towards the East Gate. The Queen stood and addressed the crowd:

'The time has come for our visitors to depart. Annwn will be forever grateful for what they have done. Without them I would not have been restored to you.'

A great cheer rose and echoed around the hillsides.

'Timmery and Charkle, for your bravery and fearlessness in the face of danger we give you the right to enter Annwn through any portal. Once in Annwn, you will transform again into hummingbirds. The freedom of the land beyond the four portals is yours for eternity.'

Timmery and Charkle fluttered around the Queen's head then raced around the arena whilst the crowd clapped and cheered. Once they were back on their perch the crowd became silent and waited expectantly for the Queen to continue.

'Where is Lloyd the Goldsmith?'

'I'm here, Your Majesty,' said a voice from the crowd.

A tall robed figure, with a candle in one hand and a small leather pouch in the other stepped towards the platform and bowed low before the Queen.

'We have a gift for you Jack, made by the Master Goldsmith of Annwn.'

Lloyd came and stood next to the Queen and opened the pouch. Into her hand he shook a golden acorn. Jack gasped. It was beautiful. It was the same shape as Nora's, only smaller. The stalk had been looped and a chain threaded through it. The Queen walked over to Jack. He bowed his head.

'For you, *The One*, who has saved us all, a special golden acorn. All the power of Annwn is within it. You have proved yourself worthy, a true Brenin. Annwn has been honoured to have the presence of a Brenin once again.'

As she put the chain around Jack's neck, the crowd stood.

'The Brenin, the Brenin,' they chanted.

The Queen turned to face the crowd and the chanting subsided.

'We have one more guest to honour,' she said as she walked over to Camelin. 'Is there anything we can give you as a gift?'

Camelin bowed his head and winked at Jack.

'Could I have an oracular frog? It's something I've always wanted.'

'You may. We will send someone to find one before you depart.'

Gwillam approached the Queen.

'Your Majesty, my former acolyte, Gavin, says he has an oracular frog he'd be more than happy for Camelin to have.'

'Oh! Thank you, thank you so much,' croaked Camelin.

Gavin held the jar high for the Queen to see. Inside was the little green frog. Jack wondered if Camelin was overdoing the *thank yous*, but no one seemed to suspect he'd planned the gift in advance. Gavin walked to the centre of the arena and gave the frog to Nora. She carefully added it to the other things in the Cauldron.

'It is time for The Parting of The Ways,' announced the Queen.

Gwillam banged his staff three times and when every eye was upon him he announced loudly: 'Let the procession begin.'

The people rose and filed down the hillside. The bearers of the Treasures stepped apart and began to walk towards the four corners of Annwn. People from the north followed the Spear, those from the east set off after the Stone of Destiny and the villagers from the south followed the Sword.

Jack and Camelin flew onto Gwillam's shoulders, Timmery and Charkle perched on Gavin's and they set off towards Glasruhen Gate.

Jack looked around to see who was following. Only the Queen, with Hesta and Winver perched on her shoulders, was behind them.

They followed a pathway lined with standing stones, which skirted the swamp. After a while Nora stopped and put the cauldron down.

'Gavin and I will carry that for you now,' said Gwillam.

'I think the rest of you can fly,' said Nora.

The Queen stopped too.

'Now we're away from the eyes of Annwn we can be ourselves again. Hesta and Winver, you can show Jack and Camelin the way. We'll meet you at the gate.'

The Queen raised her hands in the air and began to spin. It wasn't long before Cora, Gwen and Elan appeared.

'Follow us,' croaked Hesta.

Jack and Camelin flew after the two white ravens. They raced over the brow of a large mound and carried on towards Glasruhen Gate. Jack looked back towards the Citadel one last time before it was lost from sight. He couldn't see much except millions of bright stars in the sky and the snaking candlelit processions as the people made their ways home. He sighed. He wanted to stay but he also wanted to get back to Arrana. He couldn't wait to see her face when they showed her the acorns.

when all is equal, all is done, and joy is brought to everyone

The Brenin will be crowned again,
Over the forest he will reign.

DEPARTURES

Jack remembered the last time they'd tried to fly through the portal. It seemed like days since they'd arrived but he knew that they'd only have been gone from Earth for a few minutes. He sat with the others on the lowest branch of one of the Sentinel Oaks and watched the candlelit procession drawing nearer. He could hear distant singing from the other processions.

'We haven't heard the *Parting of the Ways* sung for a very long time,' said Hesta.

'You will come back soon, won't you?' asked Winver.

'We will,' piped Timmery and Charkle. 'We will.'

Jack and Camelin just nodded. No one spoke until Nora and Elan had almost reached the tree.

'Time to go,' said Camelin to the two white ravens. 'No time to chat now.'

Gwillam and Gavin put the cauldron down by the gate and then Gwillam turned to Nora.

'You'll write often won't you and tell me all the news from Earth?'

'I will, it won't be long until Samhain and we'll all be back again.'

'Next time you come through Glasruhen Gate there will be a proper welcome waiting for you,' said Elan.

Jack looked at her.

'Aren't you coming back with us?'

'No Jack, I'm needed here for a while. We can write though, you'll be able to tell me about all the things I'm missing.'

'But...'

'I have to stay. Cora and Gwen need me. We have work to do to put Annwn to rights again. When that work is done I'll return.'

'How long do you think you'll be gone?'

'I really don't know, but I promise I will come back. Now the portal is open I'll visit whenever I can.'

Jack felt sad. He'd miss Elan, but he understood why she wanted to stay and put things right. He remembered the gift she'd given him.

'Thank you for my beautiful golden acorn.'

'You have proved yourself worthy to wear it. The people will see you one day as you really are. When you return at Samhain, you'll take your place as King.'

'Me? King of the Festival?'

'No just King, the visiting King. You must know by now that you're *The Brenin* the prophesy foretells.'

Jack felt confused. Why did they all keep calling him *The Brenin.*

'I don't understand.'

'I thought you knew,' said Nora. 'Brenin means King. You are *The One*, the *King of the Forest.*'

'That's why you're able to harness the power of Annwn through your wand. You'll be able to do the same through your acorn. Arrana gave you her knowledge. Her power is within you, all you need to do now is to learn how to use it,' explained Elan.

'We couldn't have opened Glasruhen Gate without you, we were both too weak, but the power of Annwn is strong within you. Once you've been crowned, you can take your rightful position,' added Nora.

Jack took a deep breath. Elan and Nora's words had stunned him into silence. There were so many questions he needed to ask but he didn't know where to begin.

'It's time to go,' announced Nora. 'You four will have to fly through the portal.'

Timmery and Charkle hovered around Nora's head.

'I'd better transform you two first.'

With a flick of her wand the two hummingbirds spun around until two little bats reappeared.

'I loved being a bird,' piped Timmery. 'It was great to be able to see in the daytime.'

Gwillam hugged his sister and patted Jack and Camelin on their backs. Gavin bowed to them all. Elan also hugged Nora, then came over to the branch and stroked Jack and Camelin's feathers.

'I'll miss you both.'

Jack couldn't speak, he was fighting back tears.

'Are we ready?' asked Nora as she picked up the cauldron.

'Ready,' they replied.

'Bye,' Elan called.

Jack replied as they flew through the gateway. The green glow disappeared as the dark forest greeted them. He quickly looked around. Nothing had changed. His clothes were where he'd left them. Nora crossed the threshold. After she'd stepped off the last branch she put the cauldron down. For one last time they all looked into the green light coming from the other side of Glasruhen Gate.

'Time to hide the portal,' Nora announced as she took out her wand and pointed it at the ground before the archway where the branches lay.

The doors swung back slowly and closed without a sound. Then the Sentinel Oaks disappeared.

'Shall we go and see Arrana?'

They all agreed.

At the edge of Glasruhen Forest, Nora stopped.

'Listen, can you hear singing?'

It was the saddest song Jack had ever heard. There were no words, just a multitude of voices crying through the night. Nora looked worried.

'It's Arrana! We must hurry. Fly on ahead, we have to wake her. She has to touch the acorns and transfer her knowledge, or everything we've achieved will have been in vain.'

Jack and Camelin raced through the forest. Their wings clipped branches as they flew. They headed as

fast as they could to where Arrana stood. They didn't
see any Dryads, but the closer they got to the centre,
the louder the singing became.

They landed in front of Arrana. She was surrounded
by every kind of Dryad Jack had ever seen. None spoke
to Jack and Camelin, they didn't take their eyes off the
Hamadryad as they continued their sad song.

'Arrana,' Jack called. 'Arrana The Wise, Protector and
Most Sacred of All we have come to speak with you.'

'It's no use. You'll never wake her like that. You're
going to have to wait 'til Nora gets here. She'll have to
use her wand to wake her,' said Camelin.

Jack knew he had to do something. If the Dryads
hadn't been able to awaken her there must be a real
problem. She might even have faded away already. He
hopped over to her trunk and put his head next to it. He
listened. If he'd been a boy he'd have hugged the trunk to
let Arrana know they'd returned. He didn't want her to feel
alone. As Jack moved closer his acorn touched the bark. A
golden light shone onto Arrana. The singing stopped and
the forest seemed to hold its breath. Jack heard Arrana's
voice inside his head. He remembered she'd told him that
if he spoke with his heart she would hear him. He closed
his eyes and imagined she stood before him. He reached
out to her with unspoken words.

'Arrana, we have the acorns from Sylvana; the forest can be saved if only you will wake and touch them.'

Jack felt a stirring inside the trunk. He hopped back to where Camelin stood. A rapid movement followed. The trunk vibrated rapidly from side to side and when it stopped, in its place, the faint outline of Arrana appeared. It was hard to see any of her at all in the darkness. Jack heard the Dryads whispering then the mournful singing began again.

'Arrana,' thought Jack, 'we have the acorns, hold on a little longer. Nora's on her way.'

Jack heard Arrana's voice inside his head.

'You have done well Jack Brenin, friend to us all and rightful King of the Forest, but I grow weak, too weak to give my knowledge to all the acorns. There is no more time left, come closer, come closer.'

Jack moved towards Arrana, he heard Camelin sob as she bent forward. Her outline had almost disappeared. She pointed her finger at Jack's chest. A green light shimmered weakly until it hit the acorn around his neck. There was a burst of light, which illuminated the whole grove. The singing stopped.

'I empower you to do my work. You have the knowledge of Annwn, now I give you my final gift, the spirit of the Hamadryads. Use it wisely Jack Brenin, without you the forest will not survive.'

Jack felt hot. He fought to breathe. The acorn felt heavy around his neck. As the brightness increased it blinded him. Although he couldn't see her he could feel Arrana's presence and joy, and then there was nothing. He suddenly felt empty. The light faded and the forest was still. When his sight returned Arrana was gone. He touched the bark of the oak and found it was empty, only a hollow tree stood where Arrana had been.

'No!' cried Jack. 'No!'

The Dryads wailed. Nora appeared and rushed over.

'What happened?'

Jack choked. He couldn't speak any more.

Camelin looked at Nora.

'Arrana's gone. She's faded. We were too late.'

Jack cried silently before the empty oak. Nora put her hands on the bark then cried too. Camelin hung his head and put his wing around Jack. There wasn't another sound from the forest.

Jack had no idea how long they stood before the tree; eventually he became aware of the stillness. Nothing stirred until one of the Dryads stepped forward and bowed.

'All is not lost,' she said to Nora. 'Arrana gave the last of her power to Jack. He can save us all if he chooses.'

'Is this true?' asked Nora.

'I don't know what happened,' said Jack shakily. 'Arrana pointed to the acorn, a light exploded, and then she was gone.'

Nora turned to face the Dryads: 'Behold, The Brenin has returned, he will restore the Hamadryads to their former glory. You shall not fade away. With Arrana's gift he can breathe the life of Annwn into the acorns. The forests will flourish once more.'

Jack didn't understand. He knew Nora was talking about him but he didn't know how he was going to do all the things she was promising. How could he give life to the acorns?

Nora smiled at him.

'Don't worry. You weren't too late, you woke her in time. Only the true King of the Forest could have woken her without the aid of magic. Arrana gave you her power, she entrusted you to pass on her knowledge.'

'But I don't know how.'

'Tomorrow, everything will be made clear, but now we need to get you home. We don't want your grandad worrying about you.'

Jack took a deep breath. The Dryads began to sing again, but the song was different. The sadness was still there, but now he could also hear words of joy, about the forests and how the Hamadryads would once again protect the trees and all who lived in them. Nora took her Book of Shadows from the cauldron and tapped it with her wand. She began to read from the page where it opened:

> *When all is equal, all is done,*
> *And joy is brought to everyone.*
> *The Brenin will be crowned again,*
> *Over the Forests he will reign.*

'That's you Jack,' said Camelin.

'When Arrana's heirs are ready to replace her and carry on her work, then you will be crowned King of the Forest,' explained Nora. 'That's the last part of the prophesy.'

'But I'm just a boy,' said Jack.

'A raven boy,' corrected Camelin. 'And a Brenin. No, you're not just a Brenin, you're *The Brenin* but don't think I'm going to bow to you, not until you're wearing the greenwood crown. And don't you go getting any airs and graces either.'

'Come on,' said Nora. 'I've brought your clothes from the gateway; we need to get you home. We'll talk about this tomorrow.'

Jack could hear Nora talking to his grandad downstairs. He'd said goodnight and gone straight upstairs. He wanted to cry but he couldn't. He knew he shouldn't, he ought to be happy he'd woken Arrana in time. He felt exhausted but didn't feel tired. There were too many questions going round in his head. He was glad Orin was asleep. He undressed and got into his pyjamas. He knew he wouldn't be able to fall asleep. He took out his wand and the Book of Shadows and wrote to Elan. It was late by the time he'd answered all the questions she asked. Eventually he felt his eyelids closing. He shut his book and got into bed.

Jack was nearly late for school again. He promised Orin he'd tell her everything later. There were still some things Jack didn't understand. He spent the whole day at school lost in thought. He'd no idea what any of his lessons were about. He longed for home time, when he could return to Ewell House. Nora had promised to explain everything when he arrived. He wished Elan was going to be there. It seemed like an age until his class was dismissed.

Once he was out of school he raced to the top gate. Camelin was waiting for him in a nearby tree.

'Ready?'

'Ready,' replied Jack.

He ran as fast as he could down the back lane after Camelin and arrived, breathless, at Ewell House. Nora opened the gate at the bottom of the garden. When they were by the statues she stopped.

'This is where we need to begin.'

'Begin what?' asked Jack.

'The revival of the Hamadryad Oaks. I managed to rescue some of Arrana's sisters. They didn't fade away into nothingness like Arrana; I brought each of their spirits here and sealed each one inside a statue. I hoped one day we would have some acorns from the Mother Oak again. Once they're inside the acorns they'll be restored to their former selves. The repopulation of the forests can begin as soon as you empower each Hamadryad with Arrana's knowledge. She gave you her gift, now I have to show you how to use it.'

Jack took a deep breath. This was a lot of information to take in at once.

'You mean the statues aren't really stone?'

'I think we had that conversation the first day we met. I also said the statues weren't made from people. What I didn't tell you was that each of them contained the spirit of a tree.'

Jack went over and looked closely at the statues. Their faces were similar to Arrana's.

'What do I need to do?'

'We'll need the acorns. They're in the herborium.'

Camelin flew on ahead while Jack and Nora walked slowly through the garden.

'Are you alright Jack?'

'I feel so sad inside.'

'The last few days have been a strain for all of us, but everything will be put right again. Do you remember the words I read to you last night, the last part of the prophesy?'

Jack didn't have to think too hard, he'd thought of little else all day:

'When all is equal, all is done,
And joy is brought to everyone.'

'I can remember the words but I don't really understand what they mean.'

'It means that when everything's been put right in both Annwn and on Earth, everyone will be happy again, it's referring to both worlds. Elan will sort out the problems in Annwn and it's up to you to sort them out on Earth.'

Jack blew out a long slow breath.

'Can I do that?'

'Of course you can, you're King of the Forest.'

Jack laughed.

'I still find that hard to believe. My grandad and dad are both Brenins, why weren't they chosen to be King?'

'It's to do with the time and place of your birth. Remember the prophesy? You were born in the right place, at the right time. I knew from the start you were *The One*. I knew you'd save us all.'

'If Brenin means King, does that mean my ancestors were Kings of the Forest too?'

'It does, but there's only ever been one King. It was a very long time ago now, when this Earth was a better place.'

'What was he like?'

'When he was your age, he was very much like you, except he wasn't ready to take over the Kingship until his training finished. You're special Jack, you already have the power within you.'

'Special?'

'Very.'

'What happened to him?'

'He took the Sword of Power into Annwn for safety when the Romans arrived but never came back. He chose to live out the rest of his days there in peace. His final resting place is in the mound we passed before we came back through Glasruhen Gate.'

'He was mortal then?'

'Yes, if you want to find out more ask your Book of Shadows. Now let's go and get the acorns, we've got a lot of work to do before supper.'

Camelin appeared at the doorway of the herborium.

'Supper?'

'Not yet, so don't you go getting your hopes up. You can't eat until Jack's put a Hamadryad back into each of the acorns.'

Camelin pulled a face.

'You will hurry up, won't you? I'm starving!'

MIGHTY OAKS

The first thing Jack heard when he stepped into the herborium was an angry buzzing. He looked at the jar.

'What are you going to do with Velindur?'

'First things first,' said Nora. 'Camelin's been keeping an eye on him all day while I've been busy getting everything ready for you. Velindur will have to wait; it won't do him any harm to stay in there until tomorrow. I'll drive well away from Glasruhen before I release him.'

'When will the transformation spell wear off?'

'We put a very slow release one on him. It'll be days before he's a man again.'

'I hope he doesn't come back,' said Camelin. 'He really wasn't very nice. It would have served him right if they'd made him into a wasp for the rest of his life. That's what they used to do to invaders you know, Gwillam told me.'

'You'll have to tell Jack about it another time, we have more important things to do right now. Wait here. I'll fetch my wand and Book of Shadows.'

When Nora had gone Jack peeked into the cauldron.

'Where's the frog?'

'In the garden somewhere. Nora said I couldn't keep it in the loft because it needed fresh air and somewhere nice to live, so it's looking for a new home. When you're done will you help me find it? I haven't had a chance to ask it *the important question* yet.'

'What important question?' asked Nora as she walked into the herborium.

Camelin coughed and shuffled from foot to foot.

'Er… I was going to ask Jack what kind of a crown he'd prefer. See, neither of us is too keen on mistletoe, not if Hesta and Winver are going to be around.'

Nora laughed.

'I'm afraid you're going to have to see the Dryads about that, they decide what to use. But it's traditional to have at least one sprig of mistletoe in there. I wouldn't really call it a crown, it's not like the one Velindur had. It's more of a circlet with all kinds of things woven into it.'

'I'll be proud to wear it, whatever they choose.'

Nora laid her wand on the table. Jack took his out of his school bag and waited for her to tell him what he must do.

'First I need you to pass me that box.'

Jack went over to the far end of the table where Nora had pointed. He picked up a small rectangular box which was decorated with knot-work and oak trees on its lid and sides.

'Now open it and hold it steady.'

Jack took off the lid. Inside was a piece of black velvet. Nora untied the leather pouch they'd brought back from Annwn, and gently shook the acorns into the box. They were still shiny and smooth and looked enormous compared to the small golden acorn that hung around Jack's neck.

'Shall we begin?'

Nora stood in the doorway with the box in one hand and her wand in the other.

'Bring your wand Jack and follow me. You can come too Camelin as long as you don't interrupt. This is very important.'

They followed Nora to the group of statues.

'I'll read out the names in turn from my book. For each you must hold one of the acorns in your left hand and place a finger from your right on the correct statue's lips. You will feel her spirit pass into you. When there's nothing left inside clasp the golden acorn on your chain. Think hard about Arrana and the knowledge she gave you will flow into the acorn along with the Hamadryad's spirit.'

Jack took a deep breath.

'I'm ready, I understand what to do.'

Nora tapped her wand on the Book of Shadows, it opened immediately at the page she needed.

'Groweena, The Kind, Guardian of the Wood and Loved By All,' she cried.

Nora hadn't told Jack where Groweena was. He looked carefully at the statues until he was sure he could see a faint light inside one of them. As he approached the light grew brighter. He put the finger of his right hand on the statue's lips and held an acorn firmly between the thumb and forefinger of his left hand. There was an immediate surge from within the statue. Jack could feel his finger getting hot. It was the same sensation he'd had when he'd touched the rock in front of Jennet's well. He didn't take his finger away until the last spark of light was extinguished. He then clasped the golden acorn with his right hand and held it tight. A powerful energy coursed through his veins, his body felt as if it were on fire. The golden acorn shone through his clasped fist and the Hamadryad acorn in his other hand also began to glow.

'It is done,' said Nora when the light dimmed.

Jack breathed deeply. It hadn't been an unpleasant sensation but it wasn't like any other feeling he'd ever had.

'What do I do with the acorn now?'

'I've prepared some pots by the rockery, go and push it into the soft earth then we'll do the others.'

Camelin humphed and hopped off behind the rockery. Jack presumed he was going in search of his oracular frog while they were busy.

One by one the names were called and one by one Jack transferred the spirit of the Hamadryad from the statue into the acorn along with Arrana's knowledge. He didn't stop until he'd held up the last acorn and Nora read out the name: 'Allana, the Beautiful, Guardian of the Grove, Most Kind and Wise,' read Nora.

'That's the Hamadryad from Newton Gill!' exclaimed Jack.

'It is, she was one of the last I rescued. Newton Gill will have a Hamadryad once more.'

Jack felt elated. He couldn't wait to go and see the Gnarles and tell them the good news. He quickly transferred the last tree spirit into its acorn and planted it in the last empty pot.

'Our work is done for tonight, would you like to help plant them at the weekend?'

'I would, especially Allana. I'm so pleased for the Gnarles. Does it mean the Dryads will return to Newton Gill Forest and the Gnarles won't be hollow trees anymore?'

'There's a lot of work to be done before any of the Dryads return, new trees will need to grow. Dryads won't live in a tree once it's become a Gnarle. When Allana is established the new trees will flourish again in Newton Gill Forest. The Gnarles will have lots of company and they'll never be lonely again.'

'Haven't you finished yet?' grumbled Camelin. 'I need to show Jack my oracular frog. He hasn't had a good look at him yet.'

'Him?' said Nora, 'I think you'll find *he's* a she.'

'What! I've got a girl frog? What use is she going to be?'

'*She* has a name. It's Saige.'

'I don't care what her name is, I wanted an oracular frog. Only the males predict. She's going to be about as much use as a glass football.'

Jack tried not to laugh.

'Can I go and help Camelin look for Saige?'

'Of course you can, we've done all we can for the moment. The Hamadryad acorns grow at a tremendous rate, by the weekend they'll be strong saplings, big enough to plant. In no time at all we'll have mighty oaks in the forests again. It won't be long before you'll be able to visit Arrana's little sisters.'

Camelin shuffled and gave Nora a pleading look.

'Very well, off you go, but that frog has to be back in the garden by nightfall, I'm not having you keep it in your loft.'

Nora picked up the box and went back to the herborium. Camelin didn't look too pleased.

'Have you tried asking Saige the *important question* yet?' asked Jack.

'Naw, I couldn't find him, I mean her.'

'Perhaps if we call her she might come out.'

'You can if you want.'

Jack called and called, he looked everywhere he thought a little frog might be hiding but she was nowhere to be seen.

'It's getting late. I'm going to have to go home for my supper.'

Camelin mumbled something, which Jack didn't hear. He went and said goodbye to Nora then made his way to the hedge.

'I'll see you tomorrow after school,' he called.

Camelin didn't answer, he was too busy grumbling to himself. Jack smiled as he stood and watched him poking around the flowerbeds with his beak.

After supper, Orin wanted to know all about Annwn. Jack made her promise to be surprised if Camelin wanted to tell her everything too. He was just about to get into bed when his Book of Shadows vibrated. He turned to the front page and writing began to appear. It was a message from Camelin:

Nora says 2 tell yu its party time 2morow nite
Yor grandad nows all abot it so yu can cum after schol
bring yur wellis

Jack wondered what kind of a party it was going to be, so he wrote back:

Why do I need my wellingtons?

It wasn't long before he got an answer:

> *I cant find my frog*
> *I need yu to luk in the lak*
> *Gerda too bizy to help*

Jack laughed. He read Camelin's message to Orin then replied:

> *OK*
> *I'll help you look for Saige after school.*

'I think it's time for bed now,' Jack told Orin. 'I'll collect you and the wellingtons after school tomorrow night before the party.'

Camelin was waiting for Jack by the hedge.
'Did you bring them?'
'Of course I did.'

'Put them on now and we'll go and have a look in the lake.'

They spent the next half hour hunting for the little frog, in and around the water's edge. A fluttering sound made Jack look up.

'Nora says it's party time,' piped Charkle.

Even the thought of the party didn't seem to cheer Camelin up.

'I'm sure we'll find her,' Jack told him as they walked towards the patio.

'Nora says Saige will come out when she's ready, once she feels at home. How long d'you think it takes a girl frog to feel at home? I bet it's longer than a boy frog.'

Jack changed into his shoes and they made their way to the house.

A loud cheer greeted them when they entered the kitchen. Jack took his wand out of his bag so he could understand everyone.

The rats were all seated on their upturned beakers at one end of the table eagerly waiting to hear all about Annwn. Jack looked at Elan's empty place; it didn't seem the same without her. At least Camelin cheered up when he saw the size of the rhubarb pie Nora had made.

'I thought you'd taken all the rhubarb into Annwn,' he said.

'I kept a bit back for the special celebration I promised you.'

Timmery flitted around Jack's head.

'Look at me, I'm a bird again. Nora said I could be a bird tonight so I can see what's going on and Charkle's a Dragonette again.

'It feels good to be back to normal at last,' said Charkle.'

He flew swiftly around the room. As he passed the kitchen window the last of the day's sunlight streamed in and lit up his shiny green scales. It was the first time Jack had seen Charkle look truly happy.

'Camelin look at this!' he cried, before performing a loop-the-loop over the centre of the table, blowing fire as he turned.

'Show off,' grumbled Camelin.

Nora knocked the table three times.

'I think it's time we heard all about your adventure, I wouldn't mind hearing the whole story too!'

Camelin hopped onto the table, strutted the full length of it and waited until they were all silent. He coughed twice then began.

289

'Well,' said Nora when Camelin had finished, 'that's certainly filled in a few of the missing bits for me.'

Motley stood and cleared his throat.

'Do you think there might be room for a very intelligent rat the next time you all go adventuring?'

'If we could find one,' laughed Camelin.

Nora frowned.

'There won't be any more unplanned adventures, will there?'

Jack and Camelin looked down at the table and shook their heads.

'Will there?' Nora said again to Timmery and Charkle.

'No, we promise,' they replied.

'Now, I think it's story time. Which was your favourite Charkle?'

'Oh, *The Dragon of Howling Hill*, I'd love to tell that one.'

They all clapped when Charkle reached the end of the story.

Camelin stood and stepped forward.

'How about you Timmery?' asked Nora.

Camelin sat down again.

'They'll tell all the best ones and I won't be left with anything.'

'I liked *The Rat and the Treacle Vat*.'

'What did I tell you?' grumbled Camelin, 'That's the one I wanted to tell.'

Timmery ignored him and retold the story just as well as the storyteller had. When Timmery finished, the rats cheered and shouted for more, but Nora held up her hand.

'We'll save the rest for another time. Jack needs to get home soon but the good news is he's allowed to come and stay for the weekend.'

Nora turned to Jack and smiled, he smiled back.

'Your grandad has the Allotment Club Plant Sale and will be really busy. He thought you might be bored if you had to go along. Would you like to come and stay here for the weekend?'

'I can't think of anything I'd rather do.'

'You could help me find my frog,' said Camelin.

'I will, but not tonight.'

They all said goodnight. Jack was planning to write to Elan when he got to his room but he was so tired he went straight to bed instead.

COMMUNICATIONS

There was a lot of activity in Grandad's kitchen on Friday afternoon when Jack got home from school. People were arriving with posters and trays of seedlings which they loaded into the back of Grandad's car ready for the following morning.

'Now you're sure you don't mind?' he asked Jack. 'You can come along tomorrow if you want.'

'It's fine, really.'

'I don't know what time we'll finish on Sunday, so wait at Nora's until I come for you.'

'I will, I promise.'

Jack collected Orin, put his backpack on and picked up his wellingtons. He made his way to the bottom of Grandad's garden and waved goodbye before stepping through the hedge. He felt excited. He couldn't wait to go into Newton Gill Forest and show the new Hamadryad to the Gnarles.

'You took your time,' said Camelin as Jack stepped into Nora's garden. 'I've been waiting all day for you to arrive.'

'I've been at school, I couldn't have got here any faster. Besides, I needed to get my things first from Grandad's. Look, I've brought my wellies again.'

'We can't look for Saige just yet. Nora wants to show you something.'

'Look at that!' cried Jack.

Camelin turned his head towards the pots by the rockery.

'Oh them! That's why Nora said to meet you here. That's what she wanted you to see.'

'I could hardly miss them, they've grown so much. They're like small trees already.'

Jack could see Nora hurrying from the house.

'What do you think? Aren't they wonderful?'

'They are,' agreed Jack.

Camelin hopped onto the top of the rockery.

'Have you found Saige yet?' asked Nora.

Camelin shook his head.

'You can't have looked everywhere. What about inside your secret cave?'

'Secret cave?' replied Camelin as innocently as he could.

'The one on the other side of the rockery, the one where you think I can't see you. But then, maybe somewhere that's full of crumbs wouldn't be a very nice home for a little frog.'

'There aren't any crumbs in there,' said Jack.

Camelin glowered at him, but hopped around to look inside his hidey-hole.

'She's here!'

'That's good,' said Nora. 'I'll leave you to get acquainted.'

Camelin called Jack over to pick Saige up.

'Come on, I need you to bring her up to the loft.'

'Now?'

'Right now, I can't wait any longer. The suspense has been killing me.'

Jack put his wellingtons down and carefully

scooped Saige into his hands. She croaked loudly as he held her up so he could have a good look at her.

'She's lovely. How old do you think she is?'

'Ten,' croaked Saige.

Jack couldn't believe what he'd heard.

'She is an oracular frog. Did you hear that?'

'How do we know she's ten? She could say anything.'

'Well let's test her out? Look, there are some starlings on the bird table. How many are there Saige?'

'Ten,' croaked the little frog.

'Oh great, it's the only number she knows,' grumbled Camelin.

'No, she's right, count them.'

Camelin counted the birds one by one.

'There are ten!'

'See, she is an oracular frog.'

Camelin started to jig around the rockery.

'I've got an oracular frog,' he chanted.

Jack smiled at Saige.

'What now?'

'Put her inside one of your wellingtons. We need to get her past Nora.'

Jack tipped one of his wellies on its side and Saige hopped in.

'Ready?' asked Camelin.

'Ready,' Saige and Jack replied.

Sneaking past Nora hadn't been easy. Jack hoped Saige wouldn't say anything until they were out of Nora's hearing. Camelin hopped up the ladder first and Jack followed. He pushed the wellington onto the loft floor. As he poked his head through the trap door his mouth fell open.

'Where did that come from?'

'I told you, it's that little bit of magic I tried. It's the same as the dustbin we gave to Myryl.'

'But your loft isn't big enough for anything that size, it's huge, especially where you've got it. Why didn't you put it in the middle where there's a bit more room?'

'I didn't want Nora to see it.'

'She'd hardly miss it!'

'I need you to help. I can't get the lid off so I've not been able to look inside.'

'I won't be able to get the lid off either. It's wedged between the rafter and the floor. You'll only be able to get the lid off if you make it smaller.'

'Smaller! Smaller! I'll have you know that dustbin is full of sweets. That's why I need to ask *the important question…*'

Jack interrupted Camelin.

'You do realise if Nora finds out she'll take your wand away. We've both been told to use them wisely.'

'I did use it wisely. I asked for a variety of sweets with no banana flavour.'

'Well they'll rot in there unless you reduce it.'

Camelin groaned.

'I can't bear to do it, you'll have to.'

Jack got out his wand and pointed it at the big shiny dustbin.

'*Lunio*,' he commanded.

A blue light filled the corner of the loft. Small exploding sparks crackled and fizzled as they bounced off the metal. There was a strange crunching sound as the dustbin began to shrink.

'Not too small!' yelled Camelin.

Jack didn't stop the spell until a small dustbin, an exact replica of the bigger one, stood in the corner of Camelin's loft.

'Now you can get the lid off.'

Camelin shuffled over and put his beak through the handle and flipped the lid off.

'Oh wow! Come and look Jack, I wonder how many there are?'

'A hundred and sixty two,' croaked Saige.

Jack and Camelin both looked at the little frog as she hopped around the loft.

Camelin looked disappointed.

'That's not many. You do realise I'm not going to be able to share them now, there's only going to be enough for one.'

Before Jack could reply Nora called them to come down to the kitchen.

'See you down there,' said Camelin as he hopped onto the window ledge.

'What about Saige?'

'She'll be fine, you can take her back to the garden before bedtime.'

Nora's Book of Shadows lay open on the kitchen table. She looked very excited.

'We've got a message from Elan.'

Camelin swooped onto Nora's shoulder to have a look.

'Go and sit with Jack and I'll read it out to you.'

Camelin hopped down and shuffled over to the other side of the table.

Nora sat and read:

I have wonderful news!
The Blessed Council have agreed to open all the portals.
And even better news,
Gwillam went into the mountains to the Caves
of Eternal Rest
and sent a dream message to the sleeping Druids
to tell them about my return.
They've agreed to be woken and to leave the Caves.
They want to return.
With their help, my work here will be easier than
I had expected.

'Does that mean Elan's coming back soon?' asked Jack.

'Sooner than she'd anticipated,' replied Nora. 'She'd hoped to be able to return with us after our visit at Samhain, but with the Druid's help she should be back by the summer. There's a bit more, it's a message for you Jack:

The Blessed Council has also agreed that
the ceremony for your
coronation can take place in Annwn at Samhain.

'King!' said Jack trying to get used to the sound of the word, 'I still find it hard to believe.'

After supper Nora got out her map and started to mark all the places where the Hamadryad saplings were going to be planted.

'Can we go to Newton Gill first?' asked Jack. 'I promised I'd go back and sing to them again. I don't think they were very impressed last time, it wasn't the kind of song they were expecting.'

'Of course we can, it doesn't matter what order we plant them in.'

'There was nothing wrong with the song,' grumbled Camelin. 'It was you, you're just not used to singing as a raven.'

The mention of the song jogged Jack's memory.

'I nearly forgot. I can invite two people to the end

of term concert at school when I'm performing in the choir. Will you come with Grandad?"

'I'd love to,' said Nora. 'Maybe Camelin could listen in at the door.'

'He won't have to. He can have a grandstand view; it's going to be outdoors, on the school field under the trees.'

Camelin didn't reply.

'We'll look forward to it. Now I think it's nearly time for bed, we've got a busy day tomorrow.'

They all said goodnight.

Jack had only just closed his door when Camelin appeared on the window ledge.

'Come on up, it's safe now. Nora's gone over to the lake to see Gerda and Medric to tell them all the news.'

'Safe for what?'

'Safe for you to come and get Saige and take her back to the rockery. Nora's bound to check to see she's there before she comes in.'

Jack poked his head through the trap door and put his hand out for Saige. She hopped onto it, then up his arm and onto his shoulder.

'Thanks,' said Camelin. 'See you in the morning.'

Jack smiled when he saw the group of saplings by the rockery. Their small branches were touching and he could see the leaves shaking, even though there wasn't any breeze. He knew they were talking to one another.

'I wonder how many sweets were inside the big dustbin?' he said.

Saige whispered in his ear.

'That many! No wonder he was upset!'

The little frog hopped down and disappeared into Camelin's secret cave; he'd have to find himself another place. Soon Newton Gill Forest would be alive again. Both Camelin and Peabody would have to be careful what they said or did in there in future, or Nora would know about it very quickly.

The next morning was bright and sunny; there wasn't a cloud to be seen in the sky.

'Breakfast in half an hour,' said Nora as Jack and Camelin came into the kitchen. 'It's such a lovely day I thought we'd eat out on the patio.'

Camelin groaned quietly to himself.

'I know,' said Jack once they were in the garden. 'I could transform and we could have a game of Beak Ball before breakfast, it'd give us an appetite.'

Camelin groaned again.

'What's wrong?'

'I don't feel well, I'm going back upstairs.'

'Why don't we go and sit down. You might feel a bit better after you've had some fresh air.'

Camelin sat very still and very quietly.

'Shall I go and fetch Nora?' asked Jack.

'No, but I wish I knew how long this pain in my stomach was going to last.'

'Twelve hours, thirty-two minutes and six seconds,' croaked Saige as she hopped up next to Jack.

'There are some times when you don't need an oracular frog around,' grumped Camelin. 'And this is one of them.'

'Can I do anything to help?'

'No, it's my own fault. I made a start on the sweets in the dustbin last night, I started counting them to make sure Saige was right and I sort of ate a few. I'm going to have to go and lie down.'

Camelin flew back to his loft.

'I wonder how many he ate.'

'One hundred and sixty two,' croaked Saige.

'You mean he ate them all! No wonder he's got stomach ache.'

Jack smiled, his life was full of surprises but he didn't think Camelin would ever change. He watched Saige as she hopped towards the rockery. Who would ever believe he'd just been speaking to an oracular frog!

He knew his life would never be ordinary again, not now he was a raven boy. And in a few months he was going to be crowned King of the Forest. He hoped Arrana would have been proud of him. He'd kept his promise and not let anyone down. It was going to be a long wait until Samhain, before they could go back through Glasruhen Gate. He hoped Elan would return from Annwn quickly, he was missing her already, although he didn't feel lonely. How could he with all the new friends he'd made? He felt different. He wasn't afraid any more. And with Camelin by his side, he knew he was ready to face whatever was to come.

EXTRACTS
FROM
THE

BOOK
OF
SHADOWS

To Bind The Cauldron

Lay the plates around the Yew
First the pine then Holly too.
Next the Willow and Hawthorn take,
Birch, Ash, Elm, Oak are the first eight.
Beech and Apple follow then
Now the plates will number ten
Hazel and Rowan last not least,
Now lace the Cauldron for the feast.

308

To open the Western Portal
into Annwn

The sacred wells you must locate,
From each collect a cauldron plate
When they're found and brought together
Bind them up with thongs of leather
Tap three times on the cauldron's rim
Then you'll be ready to begin
With Oak, Beech, Willow, Ash and Pine
And acorn from the Sacred Shrine
At sunset on the ritual date
Lay them before Glasruhen Gate.

INSTRUCTIONS FOR OPENING
A PORTAL INTO ANNWN

To open up a Portal wide
Into Annwn's fair countryside,
The sacred Treasure must be sought
Then before the sentinels brought.

First put five branches in a row
And say the ritual words you know.
Hold the Treasure from the shrine,
Then let the golden acorn shine.

Between the archway will be seen
A gleaming doorway, tall and green.
No humankind may enter here
Except at Samhain every year.

The Law of Annwn does decree
For trespass there's a penalty.
None may walk
through the Portal's door,
Or Annwn's Court you'll come before.

ACKNOWLEDGEMENTS

I'd like to thank Paula, Vennetta, Sue,
Dad, Molly and Geoffrey for their invaluable
contributions and encouragement.
I'd also like to say a big thank you to
Ron, for everything, and to everyone at
Infinite Ideas.